"Let's go watch the sun set." Sterling's voice was almost a whisper. Leading her by the hand, they grabbed glasses of wine and walked to the deck at the front of the boat. In silence they held hands and watched the sun make a show of its descent. Pink and orange hues, turned red and nearly purple before the sun fully tucked itself away.

Sterling led Jewel inside the cabin. They sat at the candlelit table there and enjoyed dessert. Music continued to float through the speakers in a variety of genres. They were back at love songs.

Sterling stood and held his hand out to Jewel. She took it, rose to her feet and stepped into his arms. They swayed to the soothing tempo. Jewel laid her head against his chest. His chest felt as if it were made for her to rest there. When she looked back up at him, Sterling leaned forward and captured her lips with his. When they connected, Jewel wasn't sure if the sway she felt was caused by the boat, or the dizzying affect of Sterling's kiss. He tightened his arms around her. She held him back. He kissed her breath away.

Hello Darlings,

Jump right in and journey with Jewel Chandler and Sterling Bishop through this rule-defying tale of love. You'll meet Jewel, the wittiest sister of the Chandler bunch, and Sterling, a handsome, divorced, doting father and self-made man. It's my pleasure to share their story of finding love in a place Jewel least expected. Sterling will steal your heart, and you'll find yourself rooting for them both. Jewel finally realizes that love can conquer all, including lengthy lists of highbrow standards. But when she comes face-to-face with what she had feared from the start, will they be able to work through it and find their way back to each other? Enjoy finding out!

Ciao,

Nicki

IT MUST
BE *Love*

NICKI NIGHT

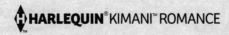
HARLEQUIN® KIMANI™ ROMANCE

Recycling programs
for this product may
not exist in your area.

ISBN-13: 978-1-335-21666-3

It Must Be Love

Copyright © 2018 by Renee Daniel Flagler

Printed in U.S.A.

Nicki Night is an edgy hopeless romantic who enjoys creating stories of love and new possibilities. Nicki has a penchant for adventure and is currently working on penning her next romantic escapade. Nicki resides in the city that dreams are made of, but occasionally travels to her treasured seaside hideaway to write in seclusion. She enjoys hearing from readers and can be contacted on Facebook, through her website at nickinight.com or via email at NickiNightwrites@gmail.com.

Books by Nicki Night

Harlequin Kimani Romance

Her Chance at Love
His Love Lesson
Riding into Love
It Started in Paradise
Desire in a Kiss
It Must Be Love

This book is dedicated to my first hero—my dad,
Benny Daniel, who first showed me what love looked like.

Acknowledgments

Sometimes, I literally feel like I'm God's favorite.
So much has transpired in the past few years, it almost
seems unfair to be so blessed. I will continue to allow him
to receive the glory for all that I've accomplished.
Without him, I wouldn't be here—writing and living
my dream. I couldn't be more grateful.

Harlequin Kimani, Glenda Howard and Keyla Hernandez,
thanks for all you do and all of your patience! To
Sara Camilli, thanks for always having my literary back.

To my family, thank you for always supporting my
#DreamJourney and for being my rowdiest cheerleaders.
We are The Freaking Flaglers! Love you Les, Lil Les,
Milan and Laila. You're my breath.
To the Daniels Clan, you're my strength.

To my sisters and brothers in the craft,
I adore and respect you. Let's keep each other lifted and
keep the books coming, Zuri Day, Tiffany L. Warren,
ReShonda Tate Billingsley, Victoria Christopher Murray,
Elle Wright, Sheryl Lister, Sherelle Green,
AD and so many more.

A special thanks to Beverly Jenkins and Brenda Jackson
for your guidance, for always being there for me and for
allowing me to drag you into stuff! LOL. I appreciate
you! Priscilla Johnson, Rowena Winfrey, Michelle Chavis,
Shavonna Futrell, Shannon Harper, Cheryl McClinton,
Stephanie Moss, Deirdre Young and Yolanda Rigby,
I can't thank you ladies enough for all of your support.
Thank you for being on my team! Shawana Kenner and
Shannel Parker, thank you for helping me name
my last two heroes!

To all my readers, thank you for being here! MUAH!

Chapter 1

"The words *Jewel* and *committed* in a sentence together…" Dominique let her statement fall and sniffed out a chuckle.

"I know. It doesn't even sound right. Ha!" Harper waved incredulously as if the concept was too ridiculous to consider.

"I'm completely capable of being in a committed relationship." Jewel defended herself, twisting her ankle in the mirror to check out the stiletto she tried on. "I just have standards."

"Standards," her friends said together and burst out laughing.

"As penetrable as a petrified forest!" Dominique's loud whisper elicited laughter from both ladies as she plopped on a pink faux fur bench with a shoebox in her hands.

Jewel placed her hand on her hip. "I am not that bad." A beat passed. "Am I?"

Dominique and Harper exchanged sideways glances and looked back at Jewel.

"There's nothing wrong with wanting certain things

in the man you date." She dismissed their unspoken scrutiny with a flip of her hand. "Why waste time getting to know someone if you know you're not compatible? I say have your fun and move on." Jewel shrugged, slipped out of the stilettos and placed them back in the box.

Leaning against the shoe rack, Dominique crossed her arms. "You don't give people a chance. Look at Maddox. He was charming and had a great body."

"Please!" Jewel twisted her lips. "I'll admit he was incredible in bed, but I don't do ex-wives. It's too much trouble." Jewel slipped her foot into a pair of sandals and tilted her head in her reflection.

"What about Sabien?" Harper closed her eyes and shook her head. "That man was gorgeous. I would never tire of that sexy accent of his."

"Boring!" Jewel sang. "And he had kids."

"That can be challenging," Dominique admitted.

"I don't think that's so bad—especially if he gets along with the child's mother."

"I prefer a man who doesn't have those kinds of attachments," Jewel said matter-of-factly.

"Oh! I know." Dominique stepped forward. "What was that guy's name?" She squinted. "Evan. That's it. He had an edge."

"Yeah, Jewel." Harper tilted her head. "What happened to him? He was really sexy."

"Oh. I remember." Dominique nodded. "He wasn't an Ivy League man."

"You're a tough one, Jewel," Harper said.

"Hey! You ladies make it sound horrible. I know you can't always help who you fall in love with so I just try to make sure I don't get too serious with anyone that I wouldn't be equally yoked with. We have to have common goals, and share similar values. I want us to enjoy certain firsts together—like our first marriage, first child, etc. I had an Ivy League education and I prefer a man who shared in that experience. What's so wrong with that?"

"When you put it that way—nothing I guess," Dominique noted.

"See. I'm not a witch. I just have standards."

"Just don't let those standards get in the way of getting a great guy. You've let a few gems slip through your fingers already, miss." Harper pointed her finger at Jewel.

"And there will always be more. Humph." Jewel put down the shoebox that she'd just picked up. "I'm too hungry to shop for shoes. Let's do this after brunch."

Without hesitation, Dominique stepped up and Harper pulled off the shoes she'd been trying on and returned them to the box.

"Good because I'm starving!" Dominique said.

The trio left the shoe store located on the main road in the Hamptons and entered the eatery that sparked their outing. Sundry's served a robust brunch with a mix of southern and French cuisine. The ladies were seated moments after entering.

Harper brought the conversation right back around after they placed orders. "Explain why Dayton didn't work again. He was an Ivy Leaguer with no kids or ex-wives."

"That man could never be taken seriously. He's more allergic to commitment than I could ever be accused of. We had our fun, but it would take a lot more to tame Dayton Rivers. Dating him was fun when it was forbidden. Now that our families actually get along, we both agree it's just not the same. Now it's like we're the best of friends."

"I don't know what's going to work for you, Jewel." Dominique took a piece of the warm bread the waiter placed in front of them and tore it in half.

"Right now, a mimosa and a—" Jewel stopped speaking. Dominique and Harper followed her gaze. The three of them watched as four handsome men passed their table following closely behind the restaurant's hostess. With seductive smiles, the men watched them just as closely.

"Whew!" Harper turned back toward the table. "With all that eye candy we just took in, I may not need dessert."

The three of them laughed.

"I'm still eating mine!" Jewel declared. They laughed harder.

Their meals arrived. The girls chatted around mouthfuls of cage-free omelets with crab and roasted asparagus, lemon brioche French toast and frittatas loaded with seasonal veggies.

"Can you believe it's already been ten years since we graduated?" Jewel sighed and sipped the mimosa the waiter placed in front of her.

"I know." Harper nodded her head. "It doesn't feel like that much time has passed."

"Dominique!" Jewel sat taller. "What's the name of that guy who had that crush on you the entire time we were in school?"

"Oh!" Harper put her hand on her forehead. "I remember him. He had a unique name."

Dominique squinted. "I can't recall his name, but I saw him a few years ago and he was gorgeous. He married some model and moved to Europe."

"Yes!" Jewel snapped her finger. "Basil!" she almost

shouted. "I went through my mental Rolodex of spices. I knew it couldn't be oregano."

Dominique's cheeks puffed. Quickly she covered her mouth to keep the champagne and orange juice from exploding all over the table. She gulped and released her laugh. The incident elicited more laughter from Jewel and Harper. Guests at surrounding tables looked over smiling as if they wished they could be part of the fun.

Wiping a tear from her eye, Harper shook her head. "We never know what's coming out of that mouth of yours."

Jewel's smile spanned wider. It took several moments for the girls to recover from another round of laughter.

"Whew!" Jewel sat back catching her breath. "I remember you refused to date Basil because he was so quiet. He was good-looking back then."

"I know, but I was afraid he'd be boring."

Jewel raised her flute as if to toast. "Yeah. That wouldn't have been fun."

"Not. At. All," Harper added.

The women became quiet for a moment as they ate and enjoyed the atmosphere. Jewel contemplated her life since high school as she absently lifted the fork to her mouth. The reunion was just a few days away. Had she accomplished all that she wanted by this time in her life? Her younger self anticipated being married by now. The mature Jewel couldn't see it since the opportunity hadn't presented itself in an appropriate enough package. Of course she'd come across a few opportunities, but now many of the gentlemen that did meet her standards were already committed or having too much fun to bother committing. She wasn't sure if she was ready for all of that anyway. She was having her share of fun as well.

"Jewel."

"Huh?" She looked up into two quizzical faces.

"You didn't hear Harper calling you?"

"What's on your mind?" Dominique put her fork down and folded her arms. "Spill it."

"I just wonder if we're going to be the only single ladies at this reunion?" Jewel sighed. *How would that look?*

Chapter 2

"When is Kylee coming?" Charles Bishop sat back in his tall chair at the head of the table. The Sunday brunch spread before him was like a feast fit for a king's court.

"In just a few weeks, Dad. School ends earlier there." Sterling sank his teeth into one of his mother's homemade biscuits and couldn't help but moan. He looked forward to his family's monthly brunch—a tradition his mother, Patricia Bishop, or Patti as most called her, started once life began to steer her adult children in varying directions. It was her way to keep them all connected.

Patti clapped her hands together. "I can't wait to see my baby girl. I think I'll take her with me to California in July. What do you think about that, Sterling? It will only be a week." Patti continued without giving Sterling a chance to respond. "Sandra's grandkids will be there too. We could take the girls to Disneyland. Yes." His mom confirmed her plan right then. "Kylee will love it. When does she have to go back to Chicago?"

"Kylee would definitely love that," Sterling's sister Taylor interjected. "I may have to go and chaperone."

"No need for you to chaperone. Sandra and I can handle Kylee and the girls."

"Not for Kylee—for you and Aunt Sandra! I know how you two get when you're together." She reached across the table and sliced the butter with a small knife and spread it across the top of her biscuit. Patti laughed and gave her daughter a dismissive wave.

"You just want to go to Disney." Sterling winked at his sister.

"You saw right through that, huh?" Taylor held her hand over her mouth and laughed. "You're never too old for Disney."

"Speaking of which. I may need to borrow Kylee a few Saturdays." Stephan's comment elicited questionable expressions from the rest of the family including Sterling. "I have a couple of events where she would prove to be…" Stephan stretched his eyes, seeming to search for the right word. "Helpful."

Taylor rolled her eyes and then directed her attention to Sterling with the tip of her fork. "Sterl, you know he intends to use your daughter to catch women, right?" She turned back to Stephan with a shake of her head. "Kids are not like carrots to a rabbit. You can't lure women with a six-year-old."

"Yes I can!" Stephan's laugh belted from his mouth. He slapped the table. Sterling chuckled and shook his head. He knew Stephan was right. He always received more attention from women when his daughter was with him.

Patti narrowed her eyes over the top of her glasses at Charles. "That," she pointed at Stephan but kept her eye on Charles, "comes from your side of the family." She swirled her finger in the air. "All that silly thinking." By now everyone at the table was laughing.

Sterling loved the camaraderie his family shared as well as the way they doted on Kylee. "I just want her to have a great summer."

"She can help me have a great summer also." Stephan raised his brow. His lips eased into a Cheshire grin.

"Really, Stephan!" Taylor huffed and shook her head.

Stephan burst out laughing again. "You all know how much I love my Kylee. Attracting women when we're together is just a perk. They love kids and dogs—especially the small ones."

"They're looking at how you interact with children and dogs. Adoration is attractive," Taylor added.

"So that's it." Stephan threw his hands in the air, feigning understanding. "It's not because they think I'm ridiculously handsome?" He laughed at his own joke. In unison, Sterling, his sister and parents just stared at Stephan for a moment before laughing themselves.

"And that part—" Charles pointed at Patti this time "—comes from your side of the family!"

"Stephan, how about getting married and having some kids of your own. I could use more grandchildren while I'm still able to hang with them."

Stephan stretched his eyes and placed a forkful of frittata in his mouth.

Patti sat back. "So how long, do y'all plan on staying single? I want more grandkids. I need other little girls to leave my clothes and jewelry to."

"She's talking to you two." Sterling pointed between his brother and sister. "I've done all of that already."

Taylor and Stephan looked at each other and at the same time, without a word they stood and began clearing the table. Charles's belly laugh could have shaken the foundation.

"You too, Sterling." Patti added with a narrowed gaze. "That marriage of yours didn't last very long and Kylee could use a few siblings."

Also without a word, Sterling got up and joined Taylor and Stephan in their silent table-clearing protest.

Now Patti laughed, loud and strong. She enjoyed teasing her kids. "Uh-huh! You all just want to deprive me. How about I help? I'll find a nice lady for you two and a nice man for you, Taylor. I have plenty of friends at work whose children are still single."

"NO!" All three shouted—hands in the air as if they could stop the comment. Their laughter joined together filling the space with an air of mirth.

Good-humored conversation continued as the family worked together to clean the kitchen and put away leftover food. Charles asked about Sterling and Stephan's technology business, which continued to grow exponentially and keep them extremely busy.

Charles then headed to the den, sat on the couch and put one foot up on the leather ottoman in the center of the room. "Y'all got time for a movie?" Charles pointed the remote at the television, clicking it to life.

"What about that movie with Denzel that was in the theaters a few months ago. I never got to see that one." Patti flopped on the couch next to her husband. Charles put his free arm around her shoulders and she nestled inside his embrace.

"Let me see if I can find it." Charles flipped through several channels on the TV.

Sterling, Stephan and Taylor finished up in the kitchen and joined their parents. During the search for the movie, the conversation somehow turned back to their single status.

"Sterling, do you think you'll ever get married again?" Taylor tilted her head contemplatively as she folded her feet under herself on the loveseat.

"Yeah. It's possible." Sterling shrugged. "My relationship with Raven wasn't horrible. We just weren't right for each other."

Sterling was seated on the other side of Patti. She touched his hand. "You tried to do the right thing, honey, and I applaud you for that."

"She was carrying your child, son. Your actions were noble," Charles added.

Sterling drew in a deep breath and let it out slowly. "Yeah. I didn't expect it to fold so quickly, but we knew it wouldn't work."

"I've always said it was best for Kylee to experience what it's like to have two happy parents living separately than two miserable ones living together." Patti nodded, punctuating her statement.

"And we all benefit from the best part of it all," Taylor interjected. "We got Kylee." She tilted her head and flashed a toothy grin.

Sterling's smile generated deep from his core. His family's support and admiration for his daughter pleased him. Taylor was right. They had Kylee—the best little girl a dad could have. She was the reason he hardly dated. If he were to bring a woman into his life, she'd have to not only accept the fact that he had a daughter, but she'd have to adore his sweet Kylee.

Sterling realized his desires might be a lot to ask of

most women and if he had to stay single until Kylee grew up, then so be it. He just hoped he really wouldn't have to wait that long.

Chapter 3

"The big guy just called an emergency meeting. He wants all of the management team in the conference room in five."

Jewel's head snapped up from her computer screen at the sound of her brother, Chris's, voice. "Did Dad say what it's about?"

Chris shrugged. "No. We just got our numbers back on track. I'm hoping it's not another chain of supermarkets closing on us."

"Please don't let that be the issue." Jewel clasped her hands together like she was praying. "That would surely impact my lofty operations goals. I've been working hard to try to impress the big guy." Jewel continued their common tease when referencing their father at work.

"I know. Being his kid offers no slack. That man can be a tyrant." They laughed at Chris's exaggeration.

Bobby Dale was no tyrant. He required excellence from his children and employees and could never be accused of giving any type of special treatment. Jewel and her siblings worked just as hard as anyone else. Adored by much of his staff, Bobby Dale created a culture where people wanted to give their best. He'd never forgotten an anniversary or birthday and had been known to jump in the trenches alongside his staff to help get a job done.

"Let's see what this is all about." Jewel grabbed a pad and pen, rose from her chair and met Chris in the doorway.

Together the two walked the corridors, ascended to the second floor and entered the executive boardroom. Midlevel and executive managers from all departments spilled into the room, taking seats around the large cherrywood table in the center of the room. Scattered small talk ensued by groups creating a low rumble until Bobby Dale's burly frame glided into the room. A hush rolled across the space, honoring his presence. His perfect posture held a well-fitting tailored suit causing him to resemble a mature model. Salt-and-pepper hair framed a strong chin as his confident stride carried him to the head of the table.

Staff made their way to the burgundy tufted leather chairs positioned against the walls and awaited Bobby Dale's announcements.

"Good morning, everyone." Bobby Dale took the seat at the head of the massive table. "Thanks for coming on such short notice."

"As if we had a choice," Jewel whispered to Chris and chuckled.

Chris snickered and cleared his throat.

"In recent months we've survived a flurry of changes in our industry, yet managed to get through them without much fallout. In light of all these disruptions, we've had to put a few things on hold, such as the revamp of our technology infrastructure and the expansion of our kitchen. Now the market seems to have stabilized and we've secured new business." Bobby Dale looked over at Chris and nodded with an approving grin. "I'm happy to report that we will be able to get back to our growth plans. But before we do that, I have a few other changes to announce."

The hush over the room deepened. Each staff member's expression matched the other.

"What's this about?" Jewel leaned close to Chris's ear.

Chris raised his shoulders and shook his head. "I was going to ask you the same thing."

"Dorothy. Will you come over here, please?" Bobby Dale called the company's chief operations officer over. Hushed voices scampered around the room as Dorothy Levy gracefully waltzed to his side. She stood next to his chair. Tall, lean and erect. Her polished appearance and chiseled features belied her warm, approachable manner. "Our dear Dorothy is leaving us."

A few gasps escaped from some of the staff.

"What? No!" Jewel tilted her head and sighed. Dorothy had been her mentor and had taught her everything she knew about being an effective operations professional.

A matronly grin spread across Dorothy's lips. Much of the staff felt the same as Jewel.

Bobby Dale lifted his hand in Dorothy's direction. She cleared her throat. "I know this comes as a shock for several of you. Believe me, it was a hard decision to make. Chandler Food Corp has been a part of my life for nearly twenty years, but the time has come for me to settle down a little. My recent health challenges have forced me into somewhat of an early retirement. However—" Her eyes washed over the room. She wore a sly grin. "You won't get rid of me so easily. I'll be around for the next month to help with the transition. Unfortunately, with the extent of my back injury, it's what I need right now. It's been an absolute pleasure working with all of you."

"You too, Dorothy," someone shouted.

A proud smile eased across her face.

"We'll miss you," someone else said.

Several employees approached Dorothy for hugs. Tears had begun to glisten in her eyes. Jewel wiped her own tears away. Dorothy had been like an aunt to her.

Bobby Dale let them all have their moment before clearing his throat and continuing with a few more announcements. When all was done, Jewel headed back to her office, shutting the door behind her. Dorothy's sudden but necessary departure and her own ambitions left her in a flux. She'd witnessed Dorothy struggle since her horrible fall the previous winter and had visited with her parents on the days Dorothy was bedridden. Apparently, the back and forth to the office along with the demands of the job had become too much for Dorothy to manage under the oppression of chronic pain. As much as she didn't want to see her go, Jewel knew that her leaving would create an opportunity for her own advancement. Surely, her father wouldn't just give her the chief operations officer title, but perhaps he'd move her into the vice president slot, which had been unfilled for months.

Jewel knew she'd invite a new level of scrutiny from Bobby Dale when she expressed her desire for the promotion. She had to convince him she was worthy of the position. And she was ready.

Jewel hit the mouse on her laptop, waking up the computer. She tapped the Word icon, opened a blank page and began chronicling her most recent accomplishments. She was going to have to make her case. Starting with the recent work overseeing the operations aspects of the new accounts they'd secured, Jewel noted all the projects she managed. Since their father had each of them spend time in various departments to assess their strengths, Jewel also made note of other areas she excelled in and how those positions helped her develop transferable skills. She sat back proudly, took a deep breath and smiled at the fact that she'd truly accomplished a lot. Dorothy had also been instrumental in her becoming such an effective manager of operations.

Jewel looked up after hearing a light tap on her door. Chris stuck his head in. "Are you going out for lunch?"

Jewel looked at the glass clock on her desk and realized how much time had passed. "Yeah. What about you?"

"Just running to get a sandwich and coming back. Wanna ride?"

"Sure." Jewel retrieved her purse from her bottom desk drawer and followed Chris through the office.

During the short ride to the deli, she contemplated telling Chris her plans for pursuing the promotion. Jewel looked out the window, but didn't seem to notice the scenery as they headed back.

"What's on your mind?" Chris maneuvered the car perfectly between the parking lines and put it in park before tuning to Jewel.

"What makes you ask?"

"I asked if you wanted to come so I could have company. You hardly spoke a word since we left the office. You're never this quiet."

Chris still hadn't made a move to exit the car. Jewel put her hand on the door handle and thought about keeping the idea scattering across her mind to herself. She took a deep breath, blew the air out and frowned.

"Upset about Dorothy leaving?"

"More than that."

"You want that VP position?"

Jewel turned to Chris. "Yes. I *really* want that VP position. I wanted it when Dorothy was first promoted to chief operations officer leaving it open, but dad didn't believe I was ready for it."

"Have you spoken to Dad yet?"

"I kind of feel like it's too soon. They just made the announcement this morning."

"So what? Let him know now. This way, Dorothy can teach you everything she knows before she leaves."

"You've got a point. I'll speak with him today."

"Good luck!"

"Thanks, lil brother." She pursed her lips. "He can't turn me down this time. I have the right qualifications, more experience and I work my behind off. I deserve that job."

Chapter 4

"You're heading to the reunion tonight, right?" Stephan stood in the door to Sterling's office with his arms folded.

"I have my ticket but I'm still working on a few RFPs I wanted to finish this week."

"You're thinking about skipping it?" Stephan entered, sat down and rested his elbow on Sterling's glass desk.

Sterling shrugged. "Maybe."

Stephan looked at his watch. "We can get those in on Monday. You haven't seen some of those people in ten years."

"I'm sure it's going to be nice, but…"

"Think of them as a room full of potential customers."

Sterling raised his brow. That made the effort worth it. Otherwise, he wasn't pressed to mingle with his former classmates from Oxford Preparatory School. Many of them were way too pretentious. He chose to drive a luxury vehicle because he liked the car, not because he needed to flaunt his wealth.

"Maybe." He finally responded to his brother, still not sounding convinced.

"Dude! Think Business. Those are wealthy people and great potential clients. If you don't go, I will."

"Your reunion isn't until next year."

"And we could have several more clients by then, if you go to yours this year. Besides, why waste the ticket? Is Noah going?"

"Of course." Sterling chuckled when Stephan mentioned his best friend since high school. "You know he's not going to miss a party."

"Then you have to go. Remember how the girls were all over you two in high school. Captain and co-captain of the basketball team." Stephan sat back, folded his arms and smiled. "Those were the days."

"Yeah, until some of them found out I was a scholarship student. I wasn't so attractive when they realized Dad wasn't paying forty thousand dollars in tuition a year. That was so ridiculous to me."

"It was, but that didn't stop you from being popular. The ladies loved Sterling Bishop! You need to go. Take plenty of business cards and treat it like a networking event."

"I guess it would be nice to see a few old friends." Sterling looked down at the proposal he'd been working on."

Stephan slipped the document from under him and flipped it back to the first page. "We'll get on these first thing Monday morning. Both of us could use the break after the hectic week we've had."

Sterling rubbed his eyes. "You're right. The words were starting to blur anyway. My eyes must be tired of reading."

Stephan stood. "Have fun. I've got a date to get ready for. Let me know how it goes."

Sterling looked at his brother sideways. Without asking, he knew Stephan's date wasn't with anyone he'd already met. Not even the one he was with last weekend. He would have called her by name.

"What? A single man can't enjoy himself?" Stephan held his hands out and snickered before leaving Sterling's office. Stephan's question confirmed Sterling's assumption.

Sterling replied with a chuckle. "Have fun, brother," he said to his back. Stephan waved without turning around.

Sterling had enjoyed several years of frivolous dating before Raven got pregnant with Kylee during their last year of college. That fun stopped when he asked for her hand in marriage. Despite the fact that the union didn't last, he was cautious about dating and didn't want to send the wrong message to Kylee by having her witness a plethora of women flowing in and out of his life. Sterling kept his dating low-key. He would only bring someone to meet Kylee if things were really serious. Kylee was the main lady in his life for now.

Sterling shut down his laptop, reached in his desk drawer and retrieved a handful of cards. Tonight would be about business. SB Tech Solutions had risen to the highest ranks of technology firms because of Stephan and Sterling's combined intelligence, fervor and savvy. The brothers wielded their smarts and charm around like magic wands. Their work and products spoke volumes and they weren't slowing down anytime soon.

Sterling met Stephan in the hallway on his way out and the two turned off the lights throughout the office before heading to the parking lot. Even now with more than thirty employees, they were still the last to leave the office on any given night.

"Let me know how it goes," Stephan said as he climbed into his SUV."

"Will do!" Sterling eased into his convertible and started the car.

Unlike Stephan, he didn't pull off right away. He started the engine, let it purr and turned on the radio while his top rolled back.

The ride home soothed him. The spring air offered just enough of a cool breeze. Sterling flipped radio stations like most men flipped television channels, taking in a variety of sounds before pulling into his driveway.

Sterling grabbed the mail from the box just before entering the four-bedroom home he'd purchased for his growing family a few years back. The day he closed was the day he and Raven had broken up. Kylee had been three years old then. Raven hadn't slept there a single night until after their divorce was finalized and the anger they harbored for one another melted away. Somehow they made their way back to being friends.

Sterling checked each room on the first floor. A habit he'd developed living alone. He smiled when he opened the door to Kylee's room. It was a snapshot of the way she'd left it when she visited for spring break. A doll lay facedown on the royal blue carpet. Stuffed animals seemed to want an escape from the hot pink toy trunk. Colorful pillows in varied sizes lined the head of the bed. Her favorite pink comforter hung slightly over the edge and a pair of fluffy slippers rested by the footboard beside a book about a princess. Sterling hadn't adjusted a thing. In a few more weeks school would end and she'd be back, filling his home with energy that only a child could stir.

It didn't take him long to shower and step into a navy blue suit and white shirt. Sterling skipped the tie, opting for a comfortable vibe. He checked his reflection and brushed at the tuft of hair resting on his chin.

Before heading out for the evening, he called Raven so he could speak with Kylee.

"Hi Dad-eeeee!"

"What's up, sunshine?"

"I have a school trip tomorrow. We're going to the museum with the dinosaurs. That's my favorite. Francesca said they scare her. I told her to just hold my hand. Mommy said she could spend the night this weekend. We're going to have so much fun."

"I'm sure you will."

"Can we go to the dinosaur museum there when I come for the summer?"

"Of course. Now tell me about your day."

Kylee went on excitedly chronicling her day from the moment Raven dropped her off at school until the second before he called her for their evening chat. By the time Kylee was done, Sterling knew what she'd eaten for breakfast, lunch, snack and dinner. He found out about the stupid boy who pushed Francesca down in the schoolyard and got in trouble and the other silly boy who had a crush on both Kylee and her best friend. Her sweet voice melted his heart.

No one knew, but he'd saved her voicemails so he could listen to that voice whenever he desired. He hated that she now lived so far from him. He never wanted his family split between homes and cherished his summers and school breaks with Kylee. Sterling wished there was a way she could stay with him even though there were zero chances of him and Raven ever getting back together. A little girl needed her mother. He could never deny the fact that Raven was a great mom.

Kylee finished speaking and huffed. Had she been talking so fast that she'd forgotten to breathe? Sterling laughed and shook his head.

"Sounds like you had a great day, princess!"

"It was okay."

Sterling chuckled. After all of that, her day was just "okay."

They ended the call in their customary way, sharing how much they loved each other and closing with a long, loud tossed kiss. "Mmmmmmmmmm-mah!"

Sterling looked at his watch and grabbed the keys to the convertible. The cocktail hour ended at nine, which gave him enough time to catch at least half of it. Sterling entered the garage from the kitchen, jumped in the car and revved the engine. He watched the garage door rise, taking note of how the moon had changed places with the sun. Sterling made his way to the country club under the flow of a silver evening light.

After pulling into the circular drive, Sterling stopped and handed his keys to the valet. Inside, hostesses directed him to the appropriate area for his event. Signs for The Oxford Preparatory High School's Tenth Reunion guided him the rest of the way. Sterling scanned the names at the check-in table to see if Noah had arrived. He hadn't. His badge was still there. Other badges bore names that Sterling could remember the faces to. He recognized one name for certain—his high school crush. That name stood out as if the letters were illuminated. Funny, he hadn't thought about her until that very moment. Sterling wondered what she looked like these days. Surely she was still pretty—probably even more beautiful now.

"Good evening and welcome to The Oxford Preparatory High School Reunion." The woman greeted him in a high-pitched voice that Sterling recognized right away.

A visual of her in frilly dresses came right to him.

"Sterling? Sterling Bishop is that you?" She shrieked.

"Emily, right?"

"Yes!" Excited, she shot up, rounded the table separating the two of them and hugged his neck.

Sterling was taken aback by her reaction. He didn't remember them interacting much back in school.

Emily released her embrace and held him at arm's length. "You are some kind of handsome, Mr. Bishop. Are you married? Have children? Do you still live on Long Island?"

The questions came too fast for him to answer. He smiled. "Not anymore. Yes. And Yes."

Emily tittered, rubbing her hands up and down his arm. "Aren't you an eyeful? Shame on your ex-wife. I would have never let you get away from me." Her smile eased into a seductive snicker. "Here." She finally released him and went back to her side of the table. "Let me get you situated." She handed Sterling his name badge and a program booklet. "This is your directory. It's complete with names, professions and business contact information from everyone in our graduating class." She tilted her shoulder forward. "My email and telephone number is on page forty-four. Feel free to use it." She winked.

"Thank you. I appreciate that," Sterling said, pinning his badge to his suit jacket. "See you around?"

"You sure will." Emily tucked her bottom lip into her mouth and shimmied. "Enjoy the party," she purred.

Sterling gave her a quick, polite nod and entered the double doors leading to the cocktail reception on the terrace.

"Sterling? Is that you?"

Sterling turned and was face-to-face with his high school sweetheart. Her green eyes sparkled and her skin glowed.

"Kirsten!" A genuine smile crossed his lips. The two hugged.

Immediately after the hug, she stepped back. Sterling noticed her swollen belly and raised a brow with a smile.

Kirsten gently placed her hand on her belly. "Yes. My husband and I are expecting…again!" Playfully she rolled her eyes. "Honey. Come." She waved a broad-shouldered gentleman over. "This is Sterling Bishop."

He pointed at Sterling before shaking his hand. "I remember you. Captain of the basketball team, right? John Wales." He pointed to himself. "From Waldorf Academy. You guys gave us a real run for our money in the playoffs our senior year."

Recognition came to Sterling right away. "John! Yes. We worked our asses off for that win. You guys weren't letting up."

"Ha! Still playing?"

"Every now and then. Good to see you and congratulations on your newest addition." Sterling gestured toward Kirsten.

The men chatted for a few moments, touching on their professions and current ventures.

Sterling got a drink from the bar and continued to mingle until he heard a familiar voice shout over the crowd. He laughed, rolled his eyes upward and looked in the direction of the obnoxious voice of his best friend, Noah.

"What's up, dude?" Noah had his arm around a woman whose neckline plunged down to her navel. He didn't bother to introduce the woman.

Sterling smiled and shook her hand anyway. "What's up, man?"

"Let's get this party started." Noah raised his drink in the air. "Oxford!" he yelled.

"Oh yeah!" Sterling and a few guys cupped their hands around their mouths and responded the way they had back in high school during games.

Noah's shout raised the level of excitement on the terrace and the chatter grew louder. Familiar faces shifted throughout the space, offering greetings and conjuring up memories of their school days. Midlaugh, Sterling's eyes landed on a stunning woman with straight, jet-black hair framing the sides of her beautiful face. The navy cocktail dress hugged her curves as if it were made right on her body.

Sterling narrowed his eyes—examining her from a distance. She held the same grace and flair from her teens. Only now it was enhanced with a womanly essence. He found himself wondering if she had married. Sterling brought his snifter to his lips and sipped. He still hadn't taken his eyes off her. In fact, he enjoyed watching her gracefully maneuver through the crowd. She moved like she had music in her flesh—flowing instead of walking, swaying with the cool breeze of the night air. Other men followed her with their eyes, too. He wasn't concerned about them.

Chimes rang, followed by a soothing voice ushering them into the main dining area so that the festivities could begin. The voice seemed like it was made just for these announcements.

Sterling watched as she swayed into the main room. The smile planted on his face was held on its own volition. She did it. She made him smile. Sterling looked at his card, checked his table number and looked for it. He put his drink down when he found his seat and then scanned the space again to find her. She was preparing to sit a few tables over. Drawn, he went to her.

"Good evening, ladies. Remember me? How are you doing? You all look lovely tonight."

"Hey, Sterling!" Dominique said.

"Good evening," Jewel said with a confident smile.

"It has been so long. How are you?" Harper chimed in.

"I'm very well." He answered the ladies but made direct eye contact with Jewel. He glanced at her left hand. No ring. Suddenly he was glad he decided to show up.

Chapter 5

Jewel wanted to look away but couldn't seem to tear her gaze from Sterling's striking hazel eyes. Good Lord that man was all kinds of handsome! Great bone structure, beautiful teeth, tall, athletic build, and now even more good-looking than he was back in school. Of course she remembered him. Sterling had matured into his manliness extremely well.

Jewel picked up the glass of ice water at her table setting and sipped. It was the only way to break the intense gaze and keep her cool. She could still feel his eyes on her. When she looked up, he wore a gentle smile, revealing those pearly whites framed by luscious lips. His erect posture exuded confidence. Jewel found that and his stylish, well-made suit sexy.

"What are you doing these days?" Harper asked him.

Jewel wished they would cut the small talk so he could walk away and allow her to breathe. Neither of them caught her drift when she fell silent. Dominique and Harper continued to engage Sterling, yet his eyes were glued to her. Jewel grew hot under the collar even though she had on a strapless dress.

She remained silent as the rest of them swapped stories about life since high school. Though she didn't partake verbally, she absorbed every word that fell from Sterling's full lips. He listened as much as he talked and Jewel liked that. Even when he spoke of his success, it didn't sound like bragging. He wasn't trying to impress them. Sterling was being himself—cool, confident.

Jewel shook her head. Why was she summing him up? She wasn't interested in this man. She continued to listen but couldn't help her muscles from tightening when Sterling pulled out pictures of his precious six-year-old daughter and spoke about his ex now living in Chicago with her. It was obvious that he was smitten by the pretty little lady with the adorable mess of curls on top of her head. Everything he'd just said made what she was feeling come crashing to an abrupt halt when he uttered the words *my daughter* and *ex-wife*. Jewel looked at the picture, offered a cordial smile and sat back, unfastening herself from Sterling's intangible draw.

She cleared her throat, which captured their attention. "Excuse me." She put the glass back down on the table.

"What about you, Jewel? What have you been up to?" Sterling's grin made her pulse quicken and she wanted to excuse herself again.

What was happening here? "Working the family business," she said as if it was no big deal that she was heir to a billion-dollar food empire.

"I see." His response felt compressed. There was so much more behind those two words. Jewel could feel it.

"Hey, ladies!" Noah stepped up, bringing a fresh wind

of excitement. His voice boomed, reaching their ears clearly over the hum of the crowd.

"Noah Hamilton!" At first, Harper parked her hands on her hips and then opened her arms for a hug.

"Long time no see, but you're all still gorgeous." He passed out hugs and kisses to each one of them.

"How's it going, Noah?" Dominique asked after their embrace.

"I can't complain. My dad always said that no one even listens anyway!

"Jewel!" Noah raised his brow. "Life's been good to you."

"Yes. Thank you, Noah. You look great!"

"You ladies wouldn't mind if I stole Sterling for a moment would you?"

"Not at all," Jewel offered up quickly.

Harper widened her eyes at Jewel. Dominique closed hers for a brief moment and sighed before chuckling. Sterling grinned.

"See you around, ladies." Sterling lifted his glass before walking off with Noah.

The second he left, Dominique and Harper looked sharply at Jewel who flopped back in her chair.

"Did you see how he looked at you?" Dominique's hand flew to her chest.

"What. Was. That. About?" Harper sat and fanned herself.

"I don't know," Jewel said.

"He wouldn't take his eyes off you, Jewel. I must say." Dominique picked up a glass of water. "Sterling Bishop has certainly grown into one fine specimen. I could see you two together," Dominique added. "He's gorgeous. You're beautiful. If the two of you walked down the street together, you'd give people whiplash from trying to look too hard. Ha!" Tickled by her own comment, Dominique actually slapped her knee.

"Sterling Bishop and I could never be an item. Did you forget he just proudly showed us pictures of his little girl and said the word *ex-wife*?" Jewel shuddered dramatically, generating another round of laughter.

"You are so theatrical," Dominique waved her hand dismissively.

"No one said you had to marry him." Harper shrugged.

"Nope. And I don't believe he's an Ivy League man, either. We're not compatible at all!" Jewel lifted her chin punctuating her summation as if the discussion was over.

Dominique twisted her lips at Jewel. "Even you don't believe that!"

Harper cackled.

"At the very least, I'd say he's great for a few dates. It doesn't have to be anything serious if you know what I mean?" Dominique winked.

"You're so bad!" Harper rolled her eyes in jest.

Jewel hadn't noticed the music playing until it was lowered and Emily took to the podium to welcome everyone and announced what was to come for the remainder of the evening.

"I bet he's the type of man that gets all into your system before you even realize you're smitten." Dominique went right back to their conversation the moment Emily walked away from the microphone.

Jewel sniffed. "I am not that gullible."

"Then go out with him. I dare you. He's obviously interested. You have nothing to lose," Dominique challenged.

Jewel bit her bottom lip and glanced across the floor to where Sterling was bent over laughing next to Noah.

"I imagine he'd be incredible in bed." The three of them giggled like they were back in high school.

After a scrumptious dinner of lobster and chateaubriand, the organizers began the program starting with an icebreaker activity. A half hour later, it was time to party.

The band played a popular song from their high school years and almost everyone hit the dance floor. Jewel, Dominique and Harper danced together in their own circle. The three weren't strangers to a party scene.

A tap on her shoulder startled Jewel. She turned around and was swallowed up by Sterling's piercing hazel eyes.

"Can I join you?"

Jewel's pulse quickened. She wanted to say no. She couldn't control this effect he had on her. Despite that, she said yes. Sterling eased his fingers between hers and they swayed to the music together. Jewel felt as if she were back in school. Sterling had never been the object of her affection then, but she felt something brewing now.

Jewel physically shook her head to shake off whatever that feeling was. She stepped back, adding space between Sterling and her, then moved in time with the lively beat. Sterling matched her step for step and before long they were engrossed in a playful battle, stirring up memories of old popular dances. Next, a song came on from their senior year. A certain dance was known to accompany the rhythm. Jewel and Sterling joined the rest of those on the floor moving along with the crowd in unison. They danced, laughed and danced more. Other songs began and ended and the two were still dancing some time later. Dominique and Harper had found partners, too, and were no longer beside Jewel and Sterling. Sweat was beginning to trickle down the center of Jewel's back. Her body had warmed from all the movement.

"Whew! I need a break." Jewel panted, threw her head back and laughed. She hadn't danced that hard in years. She felt free. "That was fun."

"Let's get a drink." Taking her by the hand, Sterling led her off the dance floor and headed to the bar. He asked for two waters and handed one to Jewel. "Want to get some air?"

"Sure." Jewel took the ice-cold water Sterling had just handed to her. She moaned after a long sip. "I needed this."

Sterling took her hand again and led them to the terrace. Jewel was hyperaware of his touch as they snaked through the crowd, but didn't pull away. She liked the way his strong, masculine hand felt wrapped around hers.

Once they hit the terrace, the cool air against her warm sweat-moistened skin caused a slight shiver. They maneuvered past people gathered in groups of two or three until they reached the far end of the terrace, which was lit mostly by the silver light of the moon. Jewel placed her hand on the marble parapet and slowly swept her gaze over the sprawling greenery of the country club and what she could see of the rolling hills on the golf course. Closing her eyes, she breathed in the fresh air, exhaling as slowly as she inhaled.

Sterling stood beside her. "Perfect night, huh?"

"Yes. It's beautiful. If my mother were here she would scrutinize every crevice of this place." Jewel turned to face Sterling and chuckled. "She's so competitive."

"So you've gotten it honestly."

"What?" Her brows creased. "Me? No."

Sterling wagged his finger. "I remember you on the

girls' lacrosse team. Unbeatable. Let's not forget the swim team," Sterling added. "Didn't you make all-county and weren't you named the scholar-athlete of the year?"

Jewel blushed. She'd forgotten all of that. "Well. Yes, there's that."

The two laughed and then eased into a sultry silence. Jewel and Sterling studied each other for a moment. The moonlight sparkled in his eyes. Jewel looked away first, turning her attention back to the lush gardens.

"Are you still as active?" Sterling asked after a while. His voice was slightly lower than the moments before.

"In the gym. Other than that, just some occasional horseback riding."

Sterling nodded. A few more moments of silence passed. "I had such a crush on you in school."

"Really?" Jewel was genuinely surprised.

"Yep. I was going to ask you to the prom, but Storm Wellington beat me to it."

"Ha! Storm." Jewel shook her head and smiled. "I haven't seen him in years."

"What ever happened to you two?"

"We dated that summer, went off to college, reconnected a few more summers and then everything just fizzled. He's in Germany now. He went there for grad school and never came back. We spoke a couple of times. He's doing well from what I understand.

"And you went to the prom with…" Jewel snapped her fingers and narrowed her eyes. "Angel?"

"Raven."

"Yes. Raven. I don't see her here tonight. What ever happened to her?"

"I married her."

"Oh." Jewel stood still, unsure of why that bit of information affected her. He'd mentioned his ex-wife inside, but hadn't said her name. The picture of the little girl with the mess of curls came to mind and she remembered Raven's face.

"She was pregnant."

"What?" Jewel was still trapped in her own thoughts.

"The summer before our senior year of college. We got pregnant. So I married her after graduation. I wanted to do the right thing."

Jewel simply raised her brows and tilted her head sideways, taking note of the fact that he'd said "we." He was a gentleman.

"It didn't last a year, but we have our beautiful Kylee. A few years ago Raven got a job offer in Chicago that offered her the opportunity to return to school and pursue her master's. Our daughter spends summers and school breaks with me until she's done with school."

"Oh. That's nice." For once Jewel didn't have much to say. She was ready to head back inside to the party, but not because she didn't enjoy being alone with him. It just didn't make sense to entertain his company any longer when she was sure it wouldn't go anywhere. "Where did you go to school?" she had to ask.

His response was all the confirmation she needed. Sterling's undergrad degree nor his MBA were earned at an Ivy League school. Jewel was far from judgmental. She still thought fondly of Sterling. He just couldn't be the one for her. She was certain that there would be areas in life where they wouldn't be able to relate. The one thing she listened to her mother about was being mindful of dating people you are compatible with. Jewel's parents were a shining example of how successful a relationship could be when two were equally yoked.

"We should head back inside. The girls are probably looking for me."

"Yeah. Noah's probably looking for me, too." Instead of moving, Sterling retrieved his wallet and pulled out a card. "I'd love to see you again. Perhaps over dinner."

Jewel hesitated just a moment, smiled and took the card from him. "Sure." She tucked it in her evening bag without looking it over.

Sterling had taken her hand again. She let him. Pulling away now would make things awkward. Their road ended there anyway. When she got home, she'd toss the card and forget about how piercing his eyes were and how his touch made her skin tingle because there was no way she could ever be with Sterling Bishop.

Chapter 6

Sterling drove to work with Jewel occupying his mind just like he had for the past few mornings. He was glad he listened to Stephan and decided to go the reunion. Seeing Jewel made it worthwhile. Sterling had also had a few inquiries about his technology service offerings since the reunion. Two meetings had already been set up as a result. His only regret was not taking Jewel's card. He'd left his with her, but she hadn't called. Sterling knew how women felt about being the first to call, but assumed Jewel was different. From what he remembered, she was a go-getter and Sterling couldn't imagine her losing that zeal. He wasn't concerned. Somehow, he'd find a way to get in front of Jewel. He had to.

Sterling couldn't pinpoint it specifically, but there was something about seeing Jewel that piqued his interest in several ways and he was determined to satisfy his curiosities about her. One night out for dinner would do it. He'd be able to determine if his interest in her was from a lingering childhood crush, or something genuinely fresh and new.

"Mr. Bishop!" The panic in his secretary Ann's voice snatched him from his thoughts of Jewel. She stood, alarming him with the speed in which she moved. "We have a situation."

"Good morning, Ann. Please continue," Sterling urged as he moved past her into his office.

"My apologies, sir. Good morning. I tried to call you and Mr. Stephan, but neither of you answered. There's a problem at our east end server farm."

Sterling pulled his phone from his belt and found that he had missed several calls, as well as text and email notifications. He wondered why he hadn't heard them. "How long ago did this happen?" His jaw clenched when he realized he still had his phone on silent from the board meeting the previous night. It was obvious that he had forgotten to turn the sound back on.

"Only about ten minutes ago. For some reason one of the backup servers seems to be shorting out. It kicks on but won't stay on."

Sterling rubbed the back of his neck. "Thank you, Ann. Let me get Stephan on the phone."

The first ring hadn't completed before his brother picked up the phone. "I know. I just finished speaking to Phil at the server farm. There was some kind of major outage in the area that was caused by a fire. They're working on getting the backups running smoothly. It keeps kicking off."

Sterling washed his hands down his face. "Steph—"

"I know." Stephan's huff was audible. "I just pulled up. I'll be inside in a sec."

Within the next few minutes every employee on deck had hands in the mix trying to get the situation rectified. Stephan kept in touch with their staff managing the server farm. Sterling was in touch with the utility company regarding the fire that caused electrical transformers to blow and affect their equipment, which housed scores of data from the customers they served. They guaranteed that services would be back up within hours.

At the server farm, maintenance staff worked hard to keep the backup servers running to avoid any major catastrophes.

Stephan walked to Sterling's office and paced. "This is all over the news."

"I know." Sterling pointed at his computer where he was watching the latest report and turned up the volume. Not one, but two major transformers had blown, causing electrical fires to light up electric lines in the area. Homes, businesses and schools in the surrounding area were all out of service. The utility company and local public service authorities were investigating to determine the cause of the problem. Stephan stopped pacing long enough to hear a few moments of the report. Sterling looked at his watch.

An hour had passed and every second counted. Their backup server was still shorting out. The team struggled to keep it up and running. Customers had the lines clogged, reporting issues with their IT systems. The entire office was in crisis management mode. Outside of Sterling's door a frenzy of people moved to and fro with an urgent pace.

"We should cancel our meetings with prospective clients today." Stephan returned to Sterling's office with his suggestion.

"No! We need to go. We'll work through this. I trust that Phil has the farm covered and he'll keep us posted. We can deal with any concerns that may come up from our prospective clients. Besides, it's important for them to know that we are able to manage a crisis and still get business done." Sterling believed in always moving forward.

"If you say so." Stephan released a heavy sigh.

Just then, Sterling's phone rang. He hesitated before answering since he didn't know the number, but picked up anyway. "Sterling Bishop speaking."

"Ah. Mr. Bishop. Bobby Dale Chandler of Chandler Food Corp here. How are you?"

"Fine, Mr. Chandler, and yourself?" Sterling stretched his eyes at Stephan. "How can I assist you?"

"A good friend of mine, Don Kota, referred me to you. You know Don, right? Kota Enterprises."

Sterling put a smile in his voice. "I certainly do. Mr. Kota is a great friend and client."

"That I know. I was speaking to him about help I was looking for and he said I should call you."

"I'm happy to be of service. Would you mind if I add my partner to the call?"

"Of course not."

Stephan eased into the chair on the opposite side of Sterling's chair. He put Bobby Dale on speaker and after introductions, they listened to him speak about the services he sought. Chandler Food Corp was looking to overhaul their entire IT system and hire his company for ongoing IT maintenance of their network.

"We can certainly do that. The first thing we'd need to do is come by to take a look at what you have in place, get a few more details and we can draw up a proposal for you," Stephan said, sounding much more cheerful than he had minutes before.

"Sounds like a plan. When can we meet?"

"If you don't mind holding for one moment, we can

check our schedules." The brothers took a few seconds to pull up their calendars and agree on a date that worked for everyone.

"Wonderful! I'll see you then. Looking forward to working with you gentlemen."

Once the call ended, Sterling and Stephan slapped a high five.

"See! Despite setbacks we have to continue moving forward."

"I'll call Phil to see if there's any progress at the farm." Stephan stood and headed for the door.

"I'll see what's happening with the utility company and check in to see about our customers who are being affected."

Despite being in the middle of their current crisis, Sterling felt better. They had a promising prospect to meet with today and now a major new prospect that also happened to be the company of the woman who recently infiltrated his curiosities. Sterling made a note to call Don, who was also his mentor, and thank him for the referral. It looked like fate was helping him get a little closer to Jewel after all.

With his brother at his side, Sterling jumped headlong back into the situation, striving to lead the company out of the problem they were facing. They ended their day with a visit to their sever farm to make sure their systems would continue working through the night. Damage to the electrical lines and transformers were still being repaired at nightfall, even though their company originally estimated it to be a few hours. News cameras captured every angle while reporters updated the public on all developments. As frustrating as the situation was for the brothers, Sterling excelled under pressure, feeding off the energy it generated. By the time he made it to bed some time in the wee hours of the morning, he felt exhausted, but also accomplished and excited about the upcoming meeting with Chandler Food Corp.

Chapter 7

Jewel took a deep breath before knocking on her father's office door.

"Come in." His voice bellowed from the other side.

Jewel tried not to let her nervousness show. Before coming to her father, she'd spoken to Dorothy, who'd prepped her to ask for the promotion. She also promised to coach Jewel and help her succeed in the position.

"Dad. I'd like to speak with you. Is this a good time?"

Bobby Dale peered over the rim of his glasses and sat back. The salt-and-pepper hairs along his temples and in his mustache gave him a distinguished look. "Anytime is a good time for you, my dear."

"This is about business, Mr. Chandler." Jewel stood straight. Bobby Dale wiggled his brows, seemingly amused by her serious demeanor. Jewel grinned letting on that she was teasing and sat.

Bobby Dale's laugh was jovial. That eased the tension for Jewel.

"On a serious note, Dad. I'd really like to talk about

the impact of Dorothy leaving and the possibility of me getting promoted to her position."

Bobby Dale slid his glasses from his face, sat back and peered at Jewel. "Go on." He encouraged her.

"Well." Jewel sat up straighter in the chair. "I know that you'll agree that Dorothy was a dedicated and accomplished leader. Under Dorothy's and your tutelage, I've had the benefit of learning what I need to know to be an effective leader in operations. I recently requested feedback from her regarding what it would take to be successful in her position and determine potential areas for growth. With that, I believe I'm well positioned to take on the position of VP of operations and would love to discuss what it would take to gain that opportunity." Jewel was relieved. She had gotten out her rehearsed speech without fumbling. She knew she had to exude confidence when speaking with her father as well as prove that she was capable and qualified.

Bobby Dale remained quiet. His expression was unreadable, which made Jewel nervous. She tried not to squirm. Jewel swallowed to keep from clearing her throat, not allowing her anxiety to show. She felt compelled to fill the silence that expanded between them. She'd played her hand. It was time for her father to play his hand and she wouldn't ruin it with anxious chatter and shoot holes in her confident exterior.

Finally, Bobby Dale pressed his lips together and nodded. "You believe you are qualified?" It was more of a statement than a question. "Tell me why."

Jewel went through the list of recent accomplishments she'd written down and practiced. Next she communicated the skills she'd developed through her experience and the impact that being coached by Dorothy had on her ability to meet and exceed the expectation of the position, resulting in positive outcomes for the company as a whole.

Bobby Dale went quiet again.

"Here's what we'll do. I will give you this new project to manage. If you prove yourself and excel in this role, within the next sixty days, we will discuss the possibility of a promotion. There's still work and growing that you'll need to do before you earn the role of VP. What do you think about that?"

"I think that's a start. Thanks, Dad… I mean, Mr. Chandler." Jewel's chest tightened. She bit back her disappointment but wouldn't let this get her down.

He chuckled. Jewel stood from her chair. She was getting that VP position. After proving herself this time, there would be no way he could deny her. Whatever this project was, she was sure she could meet and exceed her father's expectations. She couldn't wait to tell Chris about this meeting. He'd practiced with her both in person and on the phone.

"Wait!" Bobby Dale held up his hand. "We're meeting with a company tomorrow about the project I just mentioned. We need to overhaul our IT system. Clear your calendar. This company also provides consultants to manage IT and routine maintenance, which is more cost effective for us than hiring a permanent IT professional."

"Okay." Jewel nodded waiting for more information.

"They were referred to me by Don. He mentioned that they are known to be the best in the area. Dorothy will join us for the initial meeting but won't be around to manage the majority of the process. That will now be on you."

"No problem. I'll take care of it. Thank you for giving me this chance."

"You're welcome. I expect to be impressed by your professionalism."

"You got it. Thanks again." Jewel felt like pumping her fist. On the way out of her father's office, she paused and turned back. "By the way. What's the name of the company so I can do my research?"

"SB Tech Solutions."

Jewel made a mental note to look them up. She wasn't sure why, but something about the name sounded familiar. "You won't be disappointed," she told her father.

Thrusting her chest forward, she bounced back to her office. That promotion was in her hands. She sent a few emails to clear her calendar for the next day and rearranged items on her to-do list. Jewel opened a tab on her browser and was typing in the company name her father had just given her when her phone rang. She picked it up and filled her brother in on the details of the meeting with her father. When Jewel got back to her emails, she had to shift her focus to handling a contract she'd been waiting on from a new supermarket chain.

When Jewel looked at the time again, she realized it was after five. She was scheduled for a six-thirty boot camp class. With rush hour traffic, she'd have just enough time to get there, change into her workout gear and get ready for class. Her office was only twenty-five minutes away from her gym, but at this time of the day, travel times easily stretched into forty to fifty minutes.

Jewel shut down her computer, grabbed her purse and headed to the car. She double-checked that her gym bag was in the back seat before pulling out. The boot camp was hard but she made it through. She'd come out looking as if she'd traveled through rain. When class was finally over Jewel was starving. On the way home she stopped to grab something to eat. In the house, she showered, ate and pulled out her laptop to review her personal email. Moments later, she woke up and found her fingers still on the keyboard. She had fallen asleep and wasn't sure how much time had passed. Deciding to check the company out in the morning before the meeting, Jewel went to bed.

Jewel woke the next morning energized and ready for her new project. The moment she got to work, she pulled up the company name and headed to the ABOUT US section of their website. She admired the clean, sleek look and feel of the website. It was indicative of a savvy tech company. She perused the information that told of all the services the company provided. Before she could explore other sections her phone rang. Their meeting was set to take place in the executive boardroom and their guests had already arrived. Jewel realized she'd never asked what time the meeting was. First thing in the morning worked fine for her.

With her notepad, business cards and the bit of information she'd just discovered, Jewel headed to the meeting. She walked in confident, smiling and ready to impress her dad. Dorothy and Bobby Dale were already inside the room. The gentlemen they were meeting stood. When Jewel's eyes met Sterling's face the smile fell from her lips and her breath hitched. She recovered quickly enough, hoping no one noticed. But Sterling did, she could tell from the knowing grin and gleam in his piercing eyes.

Chapter 8

Sterling couldn't believe his luck. Not only did he get to see Jewel's beautiful face again, but now he had her contact information. The downside was the fact that he outright refused to fraternize with clients.

The last thing he wanted to do was create an awkward environment with a major customer. He knew that if they impressed Bobby Dale Chandler the way they had with all their other clients, referrals could potentially come pouring in. This family was extremely well connected.

By the time he and Stephan left the meeting his excitement had completely waned. There was no way he could pursue Jewel now. And if he did, he had to tread extremely carefully.

"You're quiet. What are you thinking about?" Stephan broke into Sterling's thoughts on the drive back to the office.

"Jewel." Sterling focused on the passing scenery.

"What about Jewel?"

"At the reunion, I told her that I'd like to see her again."

"So what's the problem?"

Sterling looked at Stephan incredulously. "She's a client now. That would be unprofessional."

"What's wrong with getting to know a client? No one said you had to sleep with her."

Sterling knit his brow and turned back around to look out the window. "It's not good for business."

"This job will be done in sixty days and you'll be free to date her after that."

"That could still be a problem—especially if we're providing them with ongoing technical support services. We built this company on referrals and I'd hate to work with Bobby Chandler and not be able to use him as a reference. His recommendations could guarantee us more business."

"I see what you're saying, but it seems like you're really interested in Jewel."

"What makes you say that?" Sterling asked his brother.

"You've dated a few times since your divorce, but I can't remember most of their names. Now you're contemplating waiting sixty days to make a move on one particular woman. She must be special."

"I don't know what it is, but there's something about her. I had a crush on her in high school, remember?"

"Maybe it's one of those things where you want what you couldn't have. It's not like you've ever had that problem. You've always had options whether you took them or not. I thought you were crazy when you ended things with Natalie." Stephan whistled. "That was one good-looking woman."

Sterling smiled at the memory. "She was cool, but wasn't really kid friendly."

"Oh yeah. I forgot about that." Silence took over for a moment as they listened to the purr of Stephan's luxury sedan as they drove. "How about this," Stephan said, swallowing the quiet. "Use this as an opportunity to find out more about her. By the time the contract period is over you'll know whether it makes sense to pursue her or steer clear."

"Wow. Can you believe that?"

"What?" Stephan glanced at Sterling and set his eyes back on the road before them. "Believe what?"

"You actually made some sense. That wasn't a bad idea," Sterling teased.

Stephan gave his brother a sideways glare. "I'm smart. I can run the family." He mimicked the character from one of their favorite mob movies and both of them barked out hard laughs as Stephan pulled into his parking spot in front of their office.

"Oh yeah? Well let's see how smart you are when it comes to sealing the deal. It's your turn to write the proposal. And this is a big one so give it your all."

"No worries, brother. I've got this!" Stephan pushed the driver's door open and exited. He strutted into the office ahead of Sterling who laughed all the way to his desk.

Despite Sterling's challenge to Stephan to do the proposal on his own, he met him in the conference room and the two spent most of the afternoon developing the proposal. This was a major project. Chandler Food Corp was in need of new hardware, software to manage their inventory systems and ongoing technical support. It would take a few days to gather all the estimates and information they needed to complete this proposal.

As they worked, Sterling's mind drifted back to the shocked expression on Jewel's face when she walked into the conference room that morning. He would have to keep things professional and knew it would take considerable effort.

"Who should we assign this project to? What do you think about Alex? He's one of our best account service managers and he has the right technical experience and personality." Stephan rubbed his chin.

Sterling thought about Alex, too. He would have been a great choice, but he also thought about handling this account himself. That would give him a chance to get to know Jewel. He didn't need Alex in his hair while he tried to check her out. "Alex would be good. Let's give it some more thought."

"Cool. Looks like this first draft is almost complete," Stephan said referring to the proposal. "I'll pick back up on this tomorrow. We should also have answers back on some of those estimates."

"That sounds good. I still have a ton of emails to address and a few more tasks before the day is over."

"Perfect."

Sterling stretched his neck left and then right before he closed his laptop and rose to his feet. The brothers left the conference room together and headed to their respective offices.

Sterling found that at least another thirty emails had come in while they worked on the proposal. Opening the most recent, he read it twice before he realized he hadn't absorbed a single word. He sat back and sighed. Jewel had stolen his focus. While the email before him offered no clarity, he clearly recalled the navy pencil dress that Jewel wore that morning. She looked professional, yet sexy. He remembered her slender fingers as she handed him a business card earlier. Retrieving it from his wallet, Sterling looked at the information and then turned the card around between his index finger and thumb and wondered what it would be like to date her.

Sterling had to be strategic. He decided right then that he would personally oversee this project. He'd also take this opportunity to find out more about Jewel. When the time was right, he'd take things further. In the meantime, he could find out if it would all be worth it. He'd known Jewel as a teen. She was a woman now. He could confirm if this thing he had for Jewel was the result of a lingering childhood crush or something real. He had to know if he had sensed something emotional or if this was a matter of strong physical attraction.

Sterling put in a few more hours and headed home. Inside the car, he instructed Siri to call Kylee.

"Daddyyyy!"

"Hey Snuggle Bug!"

Before he could utter another word, Kylee launched into a comprehensive recap of her entire day. Her sweet, cheerful voice accompanied him the whole way home. Besides interjecting with an occasional "really" or "wow" he barely had a chance to utter a word back.

"Mommy wants to speak to you."

"Okay, honey. Put her on." Sterling propped the phone between his ear and shoulder and unlocked his front door.

Seconds later, Raven was on the phone.

"Hi, Sterling."

"Hey. What's up?" He flicked on the kitchen light, opened the refrigerator and looked inside. The shelves were scant. He grabbed a beer, popped it open and walked to the den.

"I got accepted into one of the PhD programs."

"Wow! Congratulations. I'm happy for you." Sterling

flopped on his couch and pointed the remote at the television illuminating the room. He muted the volume.

"I'm happy, too. I'm thinking about taking summer classes to finish up so I can start in September instead of waiting until January."

"Great. I'm looking forward to having Kylee closer to home. The whole family will be excited."

"Yeah." Raven paused. "Um…that's all. Kylee's excited about coming this summer. I uh… I told her that your mother wanted to take her on a trip but I didn't say where."

"Good. Let's keep it a surprise. Everything okay?" Sterling read into her pauses.

"Sure. We're fine."

"Kylee doing okay?"

"Pfft! She's great. Can't you tell? Her recital is coming up. Will you be able to make it?"

"I plan to. Can you email me all the details so I can put it on my calendar and book my flight?"

"Okay." A few beats had passed, "Okay," she said again. "Here's Kylee."

Sterling knew Raven and he knew there was something she wanted to say to him but held back. He wondered what it was but didn't push her. When she was ready, she'd say more. Kylee was back on the phone.

"I have to eat now, Daddy. Can I call you back before bed so you can tell me another Princess Snuggle Bug story?"

Sterling's smile generated from his core. He loved that she was so excited about the silly stories he made up just for her. "Sure, sweetheart. Make sure you eat all your food."

"I will, Daddy. Love you!"

"Love you, too!"

"Muah!" Her kiss was a loud smack into the receiver.

Sterling ended the call and rested his head against the back of the sofa. Some days more than others, it broke his heart to know that his daughter resided hundreds of miles away. He'd never get used to hearing her voice without the pleasure of seeing her face unless he boarded a plane. He couldn't blame Raven for leaving. The opportunity to earn her master's degree for free while being able to still teach was perfect and better than any offer she received in New York. He was looking forward to her and Kylee returning to New York once her studies were done. September sounded much better than January. Maybe Kylee wouldn't even have to go back to Chicago when she came for the summer. Sterling would even help Raven with her move.

A low rumble rolled in his belly. Sterling got up and made a sandwich. He opened his freezer to fill his glass with ice to enjoy a cold soda and noticed his Mary Kate's apple pie—one of his favorite's from her family's company. Jewel came crashing back to his mind. He sniffed out a chuckle. That woman. What was it about her? One way or another, he was going to find out.

Chapter 9

"Let's toast to this promotion!" Dominique raised her glass. Harper joined her.

"It's not official yet." Jewel held up her finger. "I've got to prove myself first."

"That won't be a problem. Let's toast." Harper held her glass higher. "To the new VP of operations for Chandler Food Corp. Cheers!"

"Here's to moving up the corporate ladder," Dominique added.

"Wait!" Jewel held up her hand. "There's more."

"Keep the good news rolling in." Dominique put her glass down and gave her full attention to Jewel.

"So…" Jewel took a breath. "My father has given me a major project to head up and if I do well, I get the promotion."

"Whatever it is, you'll ace it, Jewel. You're such a hard worker," Harper said.

"You're such a sweetie, Harper." Jewel grinned wide. Dominique and Harper exchanged questioning glances and looked back at Jewel. "He's hired a tech company to overhaul our systems and the owner of the company just happens to be Sterling Bishop."

Dominique's mouth fell open. Harper's hand flew to her chest. Silence invaded their space for several beats.

"You're kidding." Dominique's deadpan voice disturbed the quiet. She looked toward the ceiling. "Please tell me you're kidding."

"What are you going to do?" Harper asked. Concern deepened the lines between her brows.

"There's nothing to do besides impress my dad."

"With that gorgeous piece of art around? Whew." Dominique put the back of her hand across her forehead. Harper shook her head at Dominique's theatrics.

"Business doesn't mix well with pleasure, you know," Jewel said matter-of-factly, readjusting the cloth napkin in her lap. "Especially when my dad will be breathing down my back. It's not such a big deal anyway. We're not compatible, remember?"

Harper shrugged. Dominique twisted her lips and narrowed her eyes.

"You're still on that?" she challenged Jewel.

"Of course."

Dominique leaned forward. "Didn't you say he *owned* the company that's revamping your systems?"

"Yes." Jewel wondered where Dominique was going with her questioning.

"Is the company successful?" Dominique continued her interrogation with one raised eyebrow.

"Yeah." Jewel pursed her lips. Harper looked confused as well.

"And you still feel that he's not compatible?"

"Dom. He has a kid and an ex-wife." Jewel reared her

head back as if the idea of her and Sterling getting together was absurd.

"So what. He's successful. There are plenty of great
men out there with children and exes. What's the big
deal?" Dominique dismissed Jewel's objections with a
wave of her hand and finally sipped her wine. "Are you
going to deny the fact that he's gorgeous?"

"I'll admit he's handsome."

Harper and Dominique looked at one another and
chuckled.

"He's more than handsome," Harper admitted.

"Maybe." Jewel shrugged. "Regardless. I can't date
him. I'm not interested anyway." Jewel wasn't convinced
by her own words. A quick visual of him on the night of
the reunion flashed before her. She remembered how her
pulse responded to his gaze.

"Not even once?" Dominique gave Jewel a narrowed
sideways glance.

"What for? It can never materialize into anything
more."

"That's never stopped you before and some of those
men met your standards." Dominique took a gulp of wine
and lowered her chin to her chest. "About you and those
standards…" She held a limp finger in Jewel's direction.

"I'm not giving up my standards." Jewel closed her
eyes as she shook her head. "No way."

"She's always been pretty adamant about that, Dom,"
Harper acknowledged.

"It just seems superficial to me and I know you're not
like that, Jewel." Dominique sighed.

"You're right. I'm not. If I happen to slip into a long-
term relationship, I want to make sure it's with the right
person so common ground is a must."

"She's got a point," Harper noted.

"And where has it gotten her?" Dominique shifted in her seat. "Just hear me out. It's obvious that you agree that he's good-looking, right?"

Jewel nodded.

"And successful…"

"I guess."

"You went to the same high school so that's one common experience, correct?"

"Yeah, but he—"

"No, no, no!" Dominique held up her hand. "Let me finish."

Jewel huffed. "Go ahead."

"You've dated a few other men who graduated from Ivy League schools and didn't have kids or ex-wives. Can you say that you were compatible with all of them?" Dominique raised her brow.

"That's different."

"Not really. Compatibility is about more than pedigree. Dayton had the same upbringing as you but he was completely commitment phobic and acted as if he was allergic to kids and you said that was a turnoff, remember?"

"Well…"

"Then there was William! Good-looking, Ivy League education, wealthy parents and lazy as a snail. What that tells me is that you prefer someone who has some ambition and is at least interested in having children one day. Am I right?"

"Well, yes, but—"

"Then prove to us that you're not being superficial."

Until then, Harper's attention volleyed between Dominique and Jewel. Now she nodded in agreement with

Dominique and tilted her head as she looked at Jewel, waiting for a response.

"It's not about that."

"Prove it!" Dominique sat back and folded her arms as if she'd just checkmated Jewel's king in a game of chess.

"I don't have to prove anything, but just to show you, Miss Interrogator, I will. I'm not superficial. I'm selective."

"Then go out with him, just once." Dominique challenged.

"*Maybe* after the project is complete and I'm sure after that I'll be able to report to you all the ways that we're incompatible. And then dinner will be on you! Deal?" Jewel pursed her lips and nodded.

"Deal!" Dominique clinked glasses with Jewel, sealing the deal.

"Too bad you have to wait sixty days," Harper said and the girls laughed. "Now let's toast." Harper raised her glass in the air. Dominique and Jewel joined her. They sipped, looked at each other and laughed all over again.

The girls had a history of fun challenges and this would be no different. Jewel wasn't worried. Dating Sterling for just one night would be easy. Besides the obvious, he was just like all the other attractive men she dated in the past. She would enjoy gloating with the girls after she proved Dominique wrong. There was no way that they would be compatible enough to go beyond a single date.

The girls enjoyed the rest of their dinner and Jewel headed home with the challenge on her mind. By the time she actually went on her date, she'd have a host of reasons to report on why they could never work as a couple. Working together would allow her to gather all of the information she needed to confirm her point and she would finally be done with her girlfriends questioning her standards.

Chapter 10

Sterling looked in the full-length bedroom mirror one last time before dabbing several squirts of cologne over himself. He headed out the room and trotted down the steps to the first floor of his minimally decorated townhome.

Since the work at Chandler Food Corp began, he'd taken special care in dressing on the days he visited their offices. He had never dropped in on a client as much as he did now. Today, Sterling wore a navy blue suit with a blue-and-white-striped shirt. He'd received numerous compliments with this outfit previously and found it fitting for his plans.

Sterling's "reason" for stopping by Chandler Food Corp's offices this morning was to check in on his team's efforts to preserve the company's data for transfer to the new equipment. They had put Alex in charge as the point person for the project, but Sterling still showed up frequently to review the progress. He'd even hand delivered the contract once it was signed.

After he arrived, he checked in with Alex who was

already on site. Sterling waited a while before going over to Jewel's office.

"Good morning."

Jewel flinched. "Oh! Good morning, Sterling." She looked up briefly and directed her attention back to her laptop.

"I didn't mean to startle you. I can come back another time," he said, taking notice of her pointed focus on the computer.

"No. That won't be necessary. Give me a sec." She held up a single finger. "I just need to finish this email."

Sterling leaned against the frame of the door. He watched her beautiful face when she scrunched her nose as she typed. He noted the way her fingers stilled and her eyes narrowed for seconds at a time before firing away at the keyboard again. He wondered what she thought about in those moments. His gaze washed over her from her head to mid-torso. Everything else was hidden behind the cherrywood desk.

"Ah! Okay." Jewel lifted her hands from the laptop as if the keys were hot and let them drop in her lap. She sat back. "Come on in." Jewel held out her hand, presenting the chair in front of her. "Have a seat. What's up?"

Sterling strolled into her office aware of her eyes on him. When their gaze met, Jewel averted her eyes, stood and walked over to the coffee machine propped on a wood file cabinet in the corner.

"Cup of coffee?" She kept her back to him.

"Sure." Sterling couldn't help but smile. He enjoyed the electricity in the air that their tension created. There was definitely something between them. Sterling could swim in it, float in it, tread in it. It energized him and made him relish her presence.

"I have hazelnut, French vanilla, medium roast and jet fuel."

"Jet fuel? Ha!" Sterling laughed. "You know about jet fuel?"

"Sure do. Those are usually reserved for Monday mornings."

"Or Friday afternoons after a long, crazy week."

"Exactly!" Jewel chuckled.

"I'll take the medium roast—black."

"Funny. I take mine black as well." Jewel reached for a mug from the wood stand next to the coffee machine, popped in a coffee pod and pressed a button. The hiss, dribble and gurgle were the only sounds in the room as the hot liquid filled the mugs. The strong, fragrant aroma wafted through the space.

Sterling appreciated her shapely frame in the well-fitting dress. Jewel's royal blue pumps matched perfectly as if they were made of the same fabric. He continued admiring her delicate manner as she removed one mug and filled another. When both were done, she carefully carried them back to her desk, handing Sterling one of the mugs that said No Talkie Before Coffee.

"I like this." Sterling tilted the mug as he read the words. He sipped. "Mmm. That's pretty good."

Jewel nodded in agreement and then took a careful sip. "How can I help you this morning?" Jewel placed her mug on the desk.

"I'm just here for a routine check-in. We've made considerable progress in a short amount of time."

"Does that mean you might finish ahead of schedule?"

"Possibly. Can't speak too soon." Sterling settled in the chair and crossed his legs.

"Oh. Okay."

"Do you need us to finish sooner?"

"Oh. No. I was just asking."

"Great. I'd hate to rush anything. I want you to be happy…" Sterling paused, considering the way his comment sounded and other implications it could suggest. "You're satisfaction is important to our company." He chose the rest of his words more carefully, sounding less personal.

"Thanks."

Silence descended between them for several moments, save for the sound of cautious sips.

"Did you enjoy the reunion?" he asked, sparking small talk.

"Actually, yes. More than I expected."

"Me, too. I wasn't going to go."

"Why not?" Jewel leaned in, seeming interested in his response.

"Work. I figured I could get more done. My brother convinced me to go and I knew Noah would have a fit if I didn't. But in the end… I'm glad I went. It was nice seeing people after such a long time—especially you."

Sterling noticed Jewel's throat shift like a lever as she swallowed.

Jewel tilted her head and studied him for a moment. "Are you flirting with me, Sterling?"

"Just being truthful."

"Well, just so you know, I don't mix business…" she let the rest of the clichéd comment hang.

Sterling set his mug down and held up both hands. "That's a noble principle—one that I live by myself."

Jewel shook her head and laughed. Sterling joined her before taking his mug back in his hands.

"I guess it's a good thing you ignored me that night when I told you I wanted to take you to dinner?"

She looked at him, pressed her lips into a tight smile but said nothing.

"It's cool." He jutted his chin forward. "Had that happened you probably would have been all over me and I wouldn't be able to get any work done here. I have that effect on women, you know."

Jewel's head jerked in his direction with brows knitted. He laughed hard, tickled by her reaction to his tease. Recognition sprang into her expression. She twisted her lips at first, but then joined him in his laughter.

"Now you can stop being so cordial. I knew you when you had braces."

Jewel covered her mouth, still chuckling. "You remembered those?" She threw her head back. "Ha! Watch it. I can always pull out the yearbook," she warned.

"At least I grew into my ears."

Jewel bent over laughing. "Goodness. When I look back at those photos, I just want to scream."

For the next several minutes they reminisced about high school days, joking about their former selves, recalling favorite teachers, classes and prized moments. Before long their coffee cups were empty and almost an hour had passed.

"Oh no!" Jewel looked at her watch, grabbed the journal on her desk and stood. "My meeting started three minutes ago."

Sterling rose from his seat and checked his own watch. He whistled. "I need to get back to the office. I'll send an email outlining updates and keep you posted on our timeline."

"That will be great. Thanks."

Sterling stood aside allowing Jewel to pass and followed behind her. Jewel walked him to the exit. They stood for a clumsy moment before stuttering goodbyes. Sterling held out his hand though he preferred to hug her. They'd returned to awkward professionalism, shook hands and parted ways. Despite the missteps at the door, Sterling felt great. He was on his way to knowing the current Jewel Chandler and he liked what he knew so far.

Chapter 11

The memory of Sterling's tall, handsome frame in that stylish blue suit haunted Jewel through the entire meeting and stole her focus. She could still smell the masculine scent of his cologne. She had to concentrate hard in order pay attention to all of the information swirling around her in the conference room.

When Jewel's time to contribute came she sounded robotic as she read directly from the bullet points scratched in her journal. She left no room for commentary as she usually did. The abrupt end to her report ran into a wall of silence for several seconds before her father asked if anyone had anything to add before they adjourned.

The staff dispersed and Jewel returned to her office. The moment she stepped past her doorframe, Sterling's lingering scent caressed her nostrils. He'd left more than two hours ago, but his presence remained in more ways than she cared to acknowledge. Standing still, she breathed deep, taking him in and then laughed. Why was she acting like a girl with a secret crush? Because she was.

The plush chair gracefully received the weight of her as she plopped down. She had to stop her mind from wandering into thoughts of Sterling. It had been happening since the reunion. That time outside on the balcony affected her more than she was willing to admit.

Despite the fact that they didn't have much in common, she was quite curious about Sterling Bishop. His frequent visits during this project weren't helping. She had come to know when he was coming before he showed up in her doorway. Instinctively, her core would tighten. Seconds later, he would appear at the entrance of her office, like he had this morning. Each time he would stay a bit longer. They never talked much about the work. She knew how the job progressed from Alex's comprehensive updates. They were slightly ahead of schedule and while she couldn't wait for the project to end and get her promotion, she almost didn't want it to since that would mean she'd no longer get to see Sterling's striking face on a regular basis.

Sterling's pop-ins weren't really necessary. She knew that, yet welcomed them anyway.

Jewel shook her head, physically attempting to rid her mind of Sterling. It was time to concentrate on her plans for making operations run more efficiently. She'd already gathered feedback from the rest of the operations staff on systems and their wish list for enhancements. She hoped that the unsolicited plan would show that she thought strategically and was fit for the promotion. She also included a proposal to renovate the kitchen to incorporate high-efficiency appliances, which would allow them to make more product in less time. She had already identified the companies she wanted to obtain quotes from and just needed to schedule appointments for estimates.

Her only issue was that her father hadn't given her any indication regarding what he felt about how she was doing. That made her nervous.

A tap on her door interrupted her keystrokes.

"Yes." Jewel acknowledged her visitor without looking up.

"Sorry to bother you—"

Jewel's neck snapped upward at the deep timber of Sterling's voice. Her pulsed seemed to pause. "I left a folder here earlier and finally realized that it was probably still on your desk," he continued.

Jewel recovered from the breath trapped in her chest. Her eyes moved from him to the file on the corner of her desk. She hadn't noticed it was there until that moment. "Oh. Sure." She lifted the folder. "Here you go." Her core tightened as he drew closer. That feeling was back. Maybe she was too wrapped up in her work to sense his approaching presence. Sterling took the folder and Jewel could swear she felt electricity shoot through the papers, which made the skin on her hands tingle.

"Thanks." Sterling opened the folder up and shook his head. "I didn't realize I'd forgotten it until I left for lunch."

Jewel only smiled.

"Speaking of which, have you eaten yet? There's a great Thai restaurant right up the street from here and they get the lunch crowd in and out pretty fast."

"Oh. No." Jewel waved. "I've got so much to do here, I couldn't think of stopping now. I'm in my groove with this project I'm working on." As if on cue, Jewel's stomach growled, defying her attempt to act as if she didn't need to eat.

Sterling simply lifted a brow. "Of course you're not hungry, but in case you are, the offer still stands."

Jewel's laugh tumbled out of her mouth despite her efforts to hold it in. Sterling laughed, too.

"I really do have a lot of work to do." Jewel definitely wanted to go, but knew it would be risky. How would she explain being out with Sterling to her father? Bobby Dale would certainly frown upon any kind of fraternizing. She remembered how angry he became at her brother, Chris, for keeping company with a former co-worker. He almost lost his job even though he was Bobby Dale's own son.

"I could bring something back for you."

Jewel thought for a moment. She was starving, but really wanted to get through the rest of the plan she was working on. "Okay. What do they have?"

Sterling sat down, pulled the lunch menu up on his phone and showed it to her. Jewel perused the items and made her selection.

"Good. I'll be right back." Sterling stood and began making his way toward the door.

"Wait!" Jewel reached for her purse. "I need to give you the money."

Sterling tilted his head and his blank stare let her know he had no intentions of taking money from her. "Be back soon." He turned and left as suddenly as he had arrived.

A fresh scent lingered behind once again. When Jewel was sure he was out of earshot, she sighed. "That man," she said, shaking her head. "If only…"

Jewel checked and responded to a few emails before returning to her work. By the time she'd gotten through the next few pages, Sterling was back.

Jewel looked at her watch. "You didn't eat there?"

"No, I figured I'd eat with you." Sterling placed a bag

on her desk and pulled out a take-out container, placing it next to her laptop.

Jewel wasn't sure if that was a good idea. "I don't think I'd be good company. I'm still waist-deep in this plan I'm working on. It's taking all of my attention."

Sterling paused with a second container in midair. "Sure. I understand." Despite his words, he seemed disappointed. She sensed it. He put the container back in the bag.

As much as Jewel wanted his company, she wondered about people seeing them eating together and reading into it. But now she felt bad.

"Sterling," Jewel called to him as he turned to leave. "Stay. Let's eat. I could use the break." Sterling's smile seemed to trigger a fresh flow of air in her chest. She got up and closed her office door. Jewel moved a few things aside and they spread their meal across the desk. "Let's see if this is as good as you say it is."

Sterling retrieved his meal, opened it, and the aroma of the food filled the space.

"Smells delicious."

"Wait until you taste it."

"What did you get?" Jewel peered over the lid into his food.

"Pad Thai noodles. They have the best around."

"Mmm. Looks good. I want to taste." Sterling scooped some into her container. "Want some of my rice?"

"Sure." Sterling gave her some.

Jewel took in a forkful of the noodles, closed her eyes and moaned. "That is good," she said, pointing to her plate. She tried the rice and covered her mouth as she chewed.

Easy conversation ensued as they ate. Gone was the

awkward interaction from earlier that day. Before she knew it, Sterling had her laughing between forkfuls. Her inhibitions about being with him at work waned and Jewel allowed herself to enjoy Sterling's presence. His sense of humor intrigued her and made her feel comfortable. They talked about their college years this time and Sterling shared the story of how he and his brother started their business. Jewel was impressed by his perseverance and savvy.

Jewel shared some information about the strategic plan she was working on and he offered some great insight on increasing efficiency in operations. She even pushed her food aside and took notes. By the time they were done, her admiration for Sterling had reached new heights. Not only was he ridiculously handsome, he was a brilliant businessman. His mind intrigued her as much as his good looks. By the time he left, she wondered what could come of her and Sterling Bishop. Jewel blushed, though no one else was in the room. Some of those thoughts were dangerously sexy.

Chapter 12

"Jet fuel?" Jewel held up an empty mug. She was standing in front of her coffeemaker when Sterling walked into her office.

"Is it that obvious?"

Instead of answering Sterling's question, Jewel frowned and stretched her eyes.

"I guess so," he continued. "Long day and even longer night." Sterling took a seat while Jewel prepared two cups of coffee. This had become their routine twice a week. He'd come by before heading to his own office, check in with his team's progress, and after coffee and conversations with Jewel, he'd move on with his day. They were more than halfway through their contract period and Sterling wasn't looking forward to an end.

"Wanna talk about it?" Jewel nodded toward the chair for him to sit.

Sterling drew in a breath and released it before speaking. "We had to let someone go yesterday afternoon. I hate when I have to do that."

"Oh. That's unfortunate." Jewel frowned and placed his coffee in front of him before rounding her desk to sit.

"And then I spent half the night working on a proposal for a new client so—" Sterling's words were interrupted by his yawn. He held a fist to his mouth. "Excuse me." He kept the fact that he was frustrated with his ex-wife to himself. Raven had mentioned a possible change in plans that would prevent him from seeing more of his daughter. It wasn't time for those kinds of discussions with Jewel. He was still feeling her out, though he admired much of what he'd already discovered. Sterling fell silent for several moments as he thought about his conversation with Raven the night before.

"Also, thanks for the advice. I incorporated it into my strategic plan and handed it in yesterday afternoon."

Sterling perked up. "What did your father say about it?"

"He hasn't given me any feedback yet. I've been so anxious. My dad is great at not letting on about what he's thinking. I've scheduled a meeting to get some feedback on how he thinks I've been doing in this role so far."

"I'm sure his response will be great."

"I sure hope so. I want this promotion."

Sterling watched how Jewel's demeanor changed. She actually seemed worried.

"You don't think your father will give it to you?"

"Let me explain something to you about my dad." Jewel set her coffee cup down. "He's not the typical father slash owner of a company. He offers no passes whatsoever to his offspring. If we want something, we have to work just as hard as any other employee. Shoot—maybe even harder. There will not be any handouts in Bobby Dale's enterprise."

"Wow! Sucks for you but overall, that's pretty cool."

Jewel paused with her cup halfway to her lips. "How's that cool?"

"Entitlement breeds contempt sometimes. Putting in the work builds character. We appreciate things more when we work for them." Sterling sat back and made a mental note to remember that bit of information. Bobby Dale was making sure his children developed a work ethic and character—two qualities he valued in people. He'd grown up around rich, entitled, spoiled brats and wasn't fond of many of the traits some of them exhibited. As wealthy as the Chandlers were, Jewel didn't seem to have those traits and he liked that about her.

"I have this charity golf event to attend next week. How about you join me?" Sterling hadn't considered those words before he spoke them. They simply tumbled from his mouth. "There will be a lot of executives there. It will be great for networking, and it's for a good cause." He felt the need to prove his intentions were professional. He didn't want her to think he was trying to mix business with pleasure just yet. When Jewel didn't respond right away Sterling continued speaking. "I actually met some of my current clients at this event last year."

Jewel seemed to contemplate his request. Sterling wondered what she thought. He wanted to hear her say yes. Being in her office for an hour twice a week wasn't enough to truly figure Jewel out. Though he liked what he'd learned so far, he needed more time with her.

"I'm not the *best* at golf."

"No need to be a great player. Plus I can give you some pointers. It's about the cause anyway. The proceeds support an arts organization that serves youth."

Jewel seemed to be in thought for another few moments. "What's the date?"

Sterling didn't realize he'd been holding his breath. He pulled out his cell phone. "I'll email you all the details."

"Okay. If it works with my schedule, I'll go." She shrugged. "I need to get out and network more with the business community. Dad always says that. Besides, I'm a sucker for a good cause."

"Great!" Sterling walked in tired, but Jewel agreeing to go to the charity event with him gave him energy. He looked down into his cup. He no longer wanted or needed the strong coffee. Despite that, he stood and took a long sip emptying the mug. "I need to get going. Confirm with me by email once you get a chance to look over the details."

"Okay. I can do that."

"Good!" Sterling sighed. "I don't have your cell number." He was pushing the professional boundary, but playing safely inside boundaries didn't get him this far in life. Sterling hit the icon for contacts. She'd almost agreed to attend an event him so why not ask. "Tell me your number and I'll call you. That way, you can store my number in your phone."

Jewel recited her number. Sterling smiled on the inside. No opposition met there. That was a start. After a few more weeks, he'd be free to make his next move.

He'd have to stretch his patience to survive the wait.

A knock on the open office door alerted them to Bobby Dale's presence. Jewel stiffened and stood. The atmosphere shifted immediately as if the all comfort had been sucked from the room. Sterling found himself standing straighter. This all happened within seconds.

"Hey, Dad." She turned to Sterling. "I'll look for those

documents and get back to you when I know if those dates work." Jewel had added a professional bravado to her voice with which she alerted and dismissed Sterling all at the same time. Her respect for her father was evident, but Sterling also sensed something else—perhaps a slight touch of fear.

"Sure. Actually, it should already be in your inbox." Sterling played along with her. "Good morning, Mr. Chandler." His greeting was cheerful. He stretched out his hand, which Bobby Dale swallowed in a strong shake.

"Good to see you, Sterling. I'm hearing great things about the work." Bobby Dale patted him on the back. "Looking forward to completion."

"Thank you, sir. I'm sure you'll be satisfied. I've got my top techs on this job."

Bobby Dale flashed a big smile. "That's what I like to hear."

"I'm going to get going. Jewel, Mr. Chandler." Sterling nodded toward each respectively. "Have a great day."

Sterling left Jewel's office with a smile plastered to his face, but felt as if he'd just escaped an encounter with his teen girlfriend's father. It was like they had almost gotten caught kissing. Maybe he needed to reconsider his weekly visits. It was obvious that Jewel was uncomfortable in her father's presence with him around. That thought made Sterling pause just before he pulled the car door open. Had she been uncomfortable just because of her father or because of him? For the first time he wondered, Was Jewel interested in being more than professional?

Chapter 13

The week was almost over and Sterling hadn't visited Jewel yet. She hadn't seen him since the day her father surprised them both by showing up in her office. Normally, he would have stopped by at least once. She missed their morning talks over coffee. Jewel couldn't act like she didn't understand why he hadn't returned. Her father's imposing figure filled her doorframe that day and compelled her to her feet. She hadn't realized she was standing at first. Twinges of guilt still gave her goose pimples as if she'd been caught with a boy in the house. She had to remember that she was a grown woman old enough to manage her own responsibilities.

On that day, Bobby Dale came to give her something she'd been looking for—feedback on her plan. Jewel spent the past week digging into the suggested research and making updates. She also incorporated some advice she'd previously gotten from Sterling. All the insight he'd offered proved to be valuable. As a business owner, he saw things from an operational standpoint that she hadn't even considered. Jewel respected his acumen.

Now as she put the finishing touches on her strategic plan and prepared for her upcoming meeting with her father, she wished Sterling had come today to look it over one last time. The urge to call him made her fingers itch. His number was in her phone now. She could run the changes by him and get his thoughts. Who was she fooling? More than wanting his opinion, she longed to hear his voice—that deep, rich, sultry sound. It had become familiar—soothing.

Jewel huffed, laughed and shook her head at her own pondering. "Woman, what is your problem?" she asked herself aloud.

"I've been wondering that for years."

Jewel started and looked up to find Chris stepping up to her desk. She'd been so engrossed in her thoughts that she never heard him coming.

Chris's laugh filled the room, replicating their father's. She couldn't help but laugh with him.

"What do you want, lil bro?"

"Just seeing what you were doing tonight. The band is coming through and I figured you, Dom and Harper might want to come by."

"I'm meeting an old friend for dinner. Maybe we can stop by after."

"Old friend…" Chris gave her a curious wide-eyed look.

"Not that kind of *old friend*, silly." Jewel pursed her lips at Chris. "You remember Kevin. He went to Oxford with us?" Her brows knit. "I think you may have been a sophomore when we were seniors." Chris tightened his eyes, reaching into his mental Rolodex. "Anyway." Jewel waved off his attempt to recall. "He's starting a new venture and we're going to meet tonight to chat about it. I think he's going to ask me to be on his board."

"Really? That sounds cool. Well, stop by after if you're up to it. It's a great band and the guys and I might do a little jam session."

"Okay. Besides I may need to end my day with a stiff drink after meeting with Dad."

Chris chuckled. "I know how that can be." He pressed his hands into the arms of the chair and stood. "Let me know if you're coming. I'll reserve a table."

Despite Jewel's anxious wait to meet with her dad, the rest of her day went quickly. Jewel went into his office hoping to be closer to her new position and left feeling that she was actually further away. Bobby Dale applauded her efforts but raised pointers about a few areas she needed to develop before she was ready for the title. He offered to help her in those areas and encouraged her to also pursue opportunities to engage in her own professional growth. Jewel could see where his assessment held some validity but wondered why she couldn't do some of that growing in the new position. Didn't every job come with a learning curve?

By the time Jewel reached the restaurant where she was to meet Kevin, she had to right her mind. During the entire ride, Jewel had wrestled with her father's words.

Kevin met her at the door of the establishment. "Looking stunning as usual." Kevin held one of Jewel's hands and leaned back to assess her smart business attire.

"Are you surprised?" she teased and then laughed.

"You haven't changed a bit," he said with a shake of the head.

"Nope!" she tittered. "Thanks," she added in a more

humble manner with a head tilt and smile before they engaged in a friendly embrace.

Together they walked into the teeming restaurant. The after-work crowd covered the place from one corner to the other. They had to shout over the chatter as they walked through the bar area. Luckily they were seated in Jewel's favorite spot in the back of the restaurant, which boasted a beautiful Zen-inspired garden complete with a stone statue of Buddha that stood at least four feet tall. A beautiful koi pond with a flowing fountain surrounded the statue. The noise from the bar could still be heard in the distance, but at least they didn't have to scream at each other to hold a conversation.

The waitress took drink orders and disappeared.

"So how's the new venture going?"

"Well, actually. I've discovered that there are a few holes to fill. We're going to have to add a few people to the staff."

"Growth already!" Jewel winked and held up her water glass in cheers.

"Ha! I wish. I just want everything to be in place."

"So let's get right down to it. What made you ask me to dinner?"

"You're a beautiful woman."

Jewel raised one skeptical brow.

Kevin's smile morphed into a laugh. She didn't know whether to take him seriously or not. He had been known for being a bit of a jokester. The next thought alarmed her. What about Sterling? Her mouth opened in a small gasp, but she recovered quickly enough. What did Sterling have to do with anything? Why had she thought of him?

The waitress placed two glasses of wine before them. Immediately Jewel grabbed one and sipped.

"My beauty has nothing to do with your business, Kevin."

"True, but that doesn't change the fact that I want you to work for me."

Jewel paused midsip. "Work for you?"

"Or with me…"

She put her glass down. "In what capacity?"

"We need help running operations. You could be our COO."

Jewel coughed. "As in chief operations officer?"

Kevin tightened his gaze in a questioning manner. "That's what COO stands for," he teased. "Come on, Jewel. I know you work for the family business, but have you always planned to stay there? I can make the offer as attractive as you need it to be. It's just that I know you have the experience."

Why didn't her father have this much confidence her? Bobby Dale wouldn't be happy about her leaving, especially so soon after Dorothy's departure. What was Kevin willing to offer? What would her family say? These and so many other thoughts barreled through her mind like a speeding train.

She looked at Kevin. He tilted his head awaiting her response. He wasn't letting her off the hook by breaking the silence.

"Kevin." She finally placed the wineglass back on the table. "I don't know about this."

Kevin sat back and rubbed his hands down the front of his slacks. Tucking in his bottom lip, he sat pensively and then leaned forward. "Do me a favor. Think about it. I'll email you the offer. Look through it and get back to me. I'll even make the deal sweeter if I have to."

Jewel took in a deep breath and let it out slowly. She

nodded instead of agreeing verbally. This was not what she anticipated. Thinking of all there was to consider made her feel overwhelmed. Jewel needed to run this by someone just to get her thoughts out. Options ran right past her siblings and girlfriends straight to Sterling. She wondered what he would say about the offer.

Chapter 14

Sterling pulled up to the address Jewel had given him and nodded his approval. For a wealthy heir, she didn't appear to flaunt her riches. Of course he noticed her love for a great pair of shoes. He was confident that her closet could clothe a large village, but she was an interesting combination of savvy, wit and charm and he found that refreshing.

Her house wasn't small by any stretch but it also wasn't an estate or incredibly ornate. From what he could tell, it had to have at least four bedrooms. He couldn't wait to see inside her world.

Sterling exited the car and trotted up the steps to her door. After a few quick knocks, he heard her call out "One minute."

Moments later Jewel appeared in the doorway like fresh air and sunshine in a yellow golf dress and de-signer sneakers. Her cheerful smile greeted him with a measure of warmth. The hair that usually cascaded down the sides of her face had been swept into a bun showing off every perfectly placed feature on her beautiful face.

Despite her spirited range-ready look, Sterling found her incredibly sexy.

"Hey there." She stepped aside, allowing room for him to enter.

"Good morning!" Sterling could feel the unusual wideness of his own smile. He leaned forward and kissed her cheek before taking in what he could of her stylish decor. The entrance and living room reminded him of a page in a home decorating magazine. "You look great," he said, turning his attention from inside her home to her.

Jewel clasped her hands together, tilted her head toward her raised shoulder and squealed, "Who me?" She took the hem of her dress between her thumbs and index fingers. "In this old thing." She burst out laughing.

"Yes. In those rags." Sterling replied.

"Thank you." Jewel curtsied. "That was my best Betty Boop. Now I'm spent," she said in her normal tone. He loved the raspy texture of her natural voice. It reminded him of a sensual jazz melody.

"And a fine performance it was." With feigned seriousness, Sterling started a slow dramatic clap.

"Ha! Let me grab my bag." Jewel grabbed a purse off a table near the door and pulled out keys. "Thanks for offering to drive." She locked the door behind them.

They walked along the paved, winding path back to his car. Sterling opened the door for her before rounding the front end and getting in himself. As he eased onto the road, his sports car made the ride feel like they rolled along quilts instead of asphalt. He loved how smooth the vehicle drove.

"I'm not sure my father would be happy to know I was hanging with you today. I didn't share my plans when I put in for the day off." Jewel scrunched her nose. "Not that I was ever one to ask for approval anyway. I'd rather ask forgiveness than permission. Ha!" Jewel threw her head back and Sterling's admiration for her slid up the scale a few more notches.

Jewel was a woman who lived her own terms. A bit rebellious even. He liked that.

"So you were the one who made your parents earn their parental stripes."

"You *could* say that." Jewel looked his way with wide, innocent eyes.

"I can see now that you were trouble."

"Yeah! My parents would probably agree."

"How are your siblings?"

"Chloe was the good one. She absorbed the brunt of our mishaps in an effort to always protect us from our parents supposed wrath. Her goal was to please Mom and Dad. At least until she became engaged to Mom's nemesis's spawn."

"What?" Jewel had him laughing.

"We'll talk about that another time. I was second in line and when I realized that Chloe was prone to pad us from being disciplined for misbehaving, I felt I had license to more rebellious. Chris and Jade weren't as bad as me, but they also weren't as good as Chloe. Chris had my mother wrapped around his entire hand. Forget a finger. He could do no wrong in her eyes. If he brought home a girl, which didn't happen often because he'd always been a player until he met Serenity, my mother would boast about how cute she was. If one of us girls dared to bring someone home, she'd scrutinize them within a centimeter of their lives. Chloe tried to bring home men she knew mom would approve of. The kind of guys I dated when I was younger would never have met her approval so I didn't bother. One day she asked if I actually liked boys. I laughed so hard I almost wet my pants."

Sterling was truly entertained. "So you *were* trouble. I could imagine the stories."

"Oh my goodness. This one time, I snuck out for a party and got caught because I accidently kicked the ladder over after climbing back to our room. It made so much noise crashing against the house and landing with a bang. I jumped in my bed and pulled the covers over my head. I could feel Chloe looking at me and probably shaking her head, but I refused to look back at her." Jewel paused to laugh. "Then we heard our parents running down the hall. They opened the door to our room and I held my breath. Chloe later told me that she pretended to be sleep as well. She didn't want to think about what was going to happen. My dad went outside and realized what happened and came right back to our room. He knew I had something to do with that fallen ladder. I ended up being grounded for three weeks, but I had a ball at that party."

"I bet."

"What were you and your siblings like?"

"We stayed in trouble. But I have to admit, Stephan was often the catalyst and because I was the older brother, I often got in trouble for things he did. Taylor was pretty sensible. She'd seen us get into enough trouble."

"My parents had a tighter reign on Jade because of me. Chris did whatever the heck he wanted. I hated that, which is why I acted out so much sometimes. I couldn't understand why he got to do things that we girls couldn't—especially when I was older."

Swapping stories about their childhood adventures entertained them all the way to the golf course. Sterling's side hurt from laughing at Jewel's animated stories—especially the one about her putting crazy glue on the bottom of her mother's house shoes so she couldn't come outside and find her playing in the dirt again. She was young enough to think that would keep her mom inside.

At the golf course, Sterling checked them in at registration. They were presented with a scrumptious breakfast spread of eggs, sausage, bacon, biscuits, oatmeal, fruit and yogurt, coffee, tea and various juices. Sterling introduced her to a few colleagues who had joined him at the table as they filled their bellies. The charity owner delivered a welcome address, thanked everyone for coming and bid them a great time out on the green. Soon after they were greeted by their assigned caddy and taken to their carts to begin their game.

"You said you weren't the best. I have a few tips for you."

Jewel looked at him for a moment before answering, "Okay."

Sterling wondered what that look was about, but dismissed it, counting it as an indication of Jewel's playful nature.

At the first hole, he let Jewel tee off first. He came up next to her to offer some tips on her stance.

"Show me," Jewel said.

Sterling stood behind her and leaned forward to grab hold of her club. "You'll want to hold your hands like this," he said, demonstrating and feeling the heat in his body rise from being so close to her. "Tilt the club this way and when you swing, follow through like this." Sterling lifted the club with her hands still on it and swung. "Remember, don't turn your whole body, just rotate your hips."

Jewel looked back at him over her shoulders. "Like this, huh?"

Energy transferred from her gaze to his eyes and traveled to his core. He cleared his throat. "Yes. Just like that." He held her gaze for a moment longer, gently swung the club and stepped back, offering space between them.

Jewel hit her ball and then it was Sterling's turn. His ball sailed high into the air and landed far from where they stood.

The two climbed back into the cart. Sterling was suddenly aware of how close they were. He tried not to look at the smooth caramel tone of her thighs when her dress rose as she sat. Jewel crossed her legs, advancing his view, and he wondered if she had done that on purpose. The temperature on the course seemed to rise suddenly.

At the next few holes, he gave Jewel more pointers. Each time they returned to the cart their closeness challenged his composure and he knew that Jewel was aware of the effect she had on him. Around the fourth hole, the game took an unexpected turn. All this time, he'd been in the lead. Suddenly, Jewel began hitting balls like a pro. His competitive nature rose and he challenged her play for play. Jewel hit one ball and they had to shield and squint their eyes to follow it toward the hole.

"Hey! I thought you said you couldn't play." Sterling planted his hands on his hips.

"I didn't say I couldn't play. I said I wasn't the best." After moving ahead of his score, she tossed the club over her shoulder and sauntered back toward the cart.

Sterling threw his hands up and followed her laughing, shaking his head in disbelief.

"You bamboozled me!" Sterling said as he climbed

into the cart. "I was going easy on you. It's time to really bring my game," he said.

Jewel welcomed the challenge with a confident tilt and sly smile. "Bring it on."

If Jewel knew what that comment did to Sterling's core, she might have held it behind her tongue. By now, he was completely intrigued by this funny, cunning, smart, witty, sexy woman. He hadn't had this much fun with a grown woman in years. Being with her on that course made his problems melt away. Her presence engrossed him, leaving little room for any other thoughts to take residence in his mind. Jewel was enticing every part of him.

They remained playfully competitive until the very last hole. Jewel was close to beating him, making him sweat to gain that win.

When they were done everyone returned to the dining hall for more food and the results of the raffles and silent auction. Jewel won a basket of spirits and Sterling won the bicycle branded by the company who donated it. Instead of keeping it, he offered to give it to one of the youths that the organization served. Everyone cheered when he made the announcement. Jewel also seemed pleased with his decision.

By the time they left late that afternoon, Sterling was full physically, mentally and emotionally. Jewel's presence was satisfying in every possible way and by the time he made it back to her house to drop her off, he found that he didn't want his time with her to end.

Sterling pulled into her driveway and shut off the engine. His intent was to walk her to the door, but instead they sat in the car talking a while longer.

"I'm glad I came," Jewel said. "I had a great time."

"You cheated!" Sterling teased.

"I did not!" Jewel raised her back. Her face was filled with surprise at his accusation.

"You pretended not to play well."

Jewel revealed a half smile. "That's not cheating." She hadn't denied playing him. "You still won so don't worry. Never underestimate a woman." She wagged her finger.

Once again, Sterling couldn't help but laugh. The two shared a hearty chuckle, but once it waned a tense silence filled the car. Sterling looked into Jewel's gleaming eyes. She held his gaze. For moments, they communicated without words. Though they couldn't consider being anything beyond professionals at the time, there was an unspoken understanding. Sterling hoped he had read her correctly. She was as curious about him as he was about her. Curious and ready to explore.

The silence between them grew more dense, weighted by an obvious desire. Jewel blinked, breaking their trance between one another and he marveled at her brown doe eyes. Sterling wanted to know what her lips felt like. They seemed to have a mind of their own. Longing drove him toward her. She didn't move. Sterling kissed her softly at first. Her lips made him feel as if he were dreaming on a cloud. He kissed her again and her lips parted, inviting him in. His hands followed, no longer able to resist the desire to touch her supple skin. He cupped his hand along her cheek. Jewel reached her arms around his neck. And right in the car, their yearnings took hold of them, dismissing all boundaries and professional courtesies. The kiss lasted long enough for them to force themselves apart to breathe. Jewel touched her kiss-swollen lips.

"I'd better go."

With that she was out of the car. Her exit was like a

sweep of wind. Sterling blinked and she was already at her door, turning her key. She waved goodbye and disappeared into the house.

Sterling sighed and let his head fall against the headrest. He knew everything he needed to know about Jewel to know that he wanted her.

Chapter 15

"How's the work going?" Dominique asked.

"Yeah, Jewel. Are you guys making good progress?" Harper added.

"At the office? Yes."

"Wait! What's that supposed to mean?" Dominique asked.

Jewel giggled. She loved teasing. "Nothing." She swirled around in her office chair with the phone pressed between her ear and shoulder. "They're finishing up now. After a few days and a couple more tests, they should be packing up."

"Is Sterling still showing up at your office all the time?" Dominique asked.

"No. I actually started looking forward to his visits. Can you believe that?" Jewel wouldn't let on just how much she'd missed seeing him. They had spoken on the phone and exchanged texts, but she hadn't laid eyes on him since the golf event.

"Mmm-hmm." Dominique moaned. "I knew you

wouldn't be able to take all that handsomeness in your face without softening on your stance."

Jewel got up to close her office door and sat back down. "He invited me to an event."

"Really!" Harper squealed.

"What kind of event?" Dominique seemed hungry for more.

"A charity golf tournament."

"Did you let him win?" Dominique asked in a tone that suggested she already knew the answer.

"He earned his win. Ha! Came this close to losing." Jewel held her thumb and forefinger a short distance apart. "He said I cheated." Jewel threw her head back and belted out a laugh.

"I knew it," Dominique said. "Sooner or later these men will learn not to underestimate us women." All three snickered.

Especially Chandler women. Jewel hadn't bothered to voice that last thought. Bobby Dale made sure his children had well-rounded experiences. They skied, golfed, played chess, changed tires, took karate classes, sailed boats, and so much more.

"What did you do after the golf tournament?" Dominique was fishing.

"Nothing." Jewel knew she wanted to hear more. For a moment she thought about whether or not she should share how they'd connected.

"Nothing?" Dominique asked incredulously.

"Aww. I was hoping there would be more." Harper groaned.

"No kiss?" Dominique nearly growled.

"Dom! It was a charity event. Not a date." Jewel decided she wasn't ready to admit more. Mentioning how much she thought of him and how often she wanted to call just to hear him talk would force her to acknowledge how much of an effect he had on her.

"So! He drove you home, right? Not to the office. You guys didn't even share a friendly hug? I'm so disappointed." Dominique snickered. "I was hoping you had a juicier story to share."

The three ladies cracked up laughing again.

"What do you want to happen here, Dom?" Jewel asked outright.

"I want you to stop acting like that man isn't handsome enough to make you second-guess your crazy standards. Shoot! Had he looked at me the way he looked at you that night of the reunion with this gorgeous hazel orbs, I'd be planning my wedding date and would be half pregnant by now."

"Ha!" Jewel's laugh was like a sharp bark. It melded with Harper's who now sounded like she was hyperventilating.

"You're nuts, Dom!" Harper laughed again. "Half pregnant," she repeated.

"You can't convince me that he has no effect on you, Jewel. Keep being around him and you'll loosen your standards soon enough. All that handsomeness is probably illegal somewhere in the world. Right, Harper?"

"The handsomeness is great, but who said I was softening on my stance. I still have my standards and that's not changing."

"I just think that's so superficial, Jewel. There are plenty of great men out there who don't have Ivy League degrees. Heck! Some don't even have degrees at all! That doesn't mean they aren't successful. There's nothing wrong with men like that, especially if he's a nice guy with goals." Dominique was on her pedestal again.

"Dom's got a point, Jewel."

"A nice guy with goals? Degree or not that sounds like a snore. Picture me gagging." Jewel pretended to put a finger in her mouth and made gagging sounds.

Harper giggled.

"That did sound a little boring, but you know what I mean. Would you preferred I say he's the type to bark 'Me Tarzan, you Jane,' grab you by the hair, lay you on his rock bed and make passionate love to you? Would it matter if Tarzan had an Ivy League education?"

"Does Tarzan also have a six-pack to go with that bed of rocks?" It took a few minutes and several fresh bouts of laughter before the girls recovered from Jewel's comment. "I didn't say there was anything wrong with him. We're simply not compatible."

"I still believe you're being superficial." Dominique was firm.

"I don't."

"Like I said before—prove it," Dominique challenged.

"What?" Jewel waved her off as if she could see her.

"Just go out on one date with him."

"Here you go again." Jewel rolled her eyes upward. "Please tell me what you think going out with him is going to prove?"

"That you're not discriminating against him because he's not what you would consider *on your level*. It's just one date. As easy as he is on the eyes that shouldn't be so hard."

"She's got a point." Harper's voice reminded Jewel that she was still on the line.

"Listen, ladies." There was a knock at Jewel's door.

"Hold on a sec." She placed her hand over the receiver. "Come in," she sang.

Chris stuck his head around the door. "I need to talk to you." The look on his face made Jewel think whatever he wanted to discuss was urgent.

Jewel looked at her watch. "Give me about five minutes."

"Cool! Come down to my office."

"Okay."

Chris shut the door. When Jewel was sure he'd stepped far enough away, she went back to her conversation.

"Ladies. I don't have a problem with Sterling. Yes, he is handsome. And now that I've gotten to know him a little more, I think he's a cool guy, but the fact remains that we're not compatible. A date won't change that."

"Aren't you even curious?" Harper asked.

"It won't matter." Jewel shrugged as if they could see her. "Besides, I could never go out with him while he's doing work for my company."

"So go when the project is complete, like you said before."

"Harper! Dominique has dragged you into her den of silliness. I wasn't serious."

"One date!" Dominique challenged again.

"Just one," Harper whined.

"You know what…just to prove you ladies wrong, when this job is over, I *will* let him take me out on one date and when I prove that we're not compatible, I don't want to hear any more of this dating stuff from you two."

"We'll be waiting." Harper snickered.

"Maybe he'll at least be a great lay."

"Dom!" Jewel and Harper yelled her name at the same time. Again, all three laughed hard.

When Jewel caught her breath, she said her goodbyes and headed to her brother's office.

"Hey, dude. What's up?" Jewel walked in and hiked half her backside onto the corner of Chris's desk.

"You're not thinking about leaving the company are you?" Chris studied her with a tight gaze.

Jewel jerked her head back. "Where'd you get that from?"

"I hear things, Jewel." He sat back in his chair.

She studied him for a moment. He looked concerned, but not angry. "Who told you?"

"I ran into Kevin." Chris learned forward and looked Jewel directly in the eye. "Are you considering this?"

Jewel huffed, moved off the desk and paced a few steps. She walked over to Chris's office door, shut it and sat down in one of the chairs facing him. She contemplated her words before speaking.

"I only looked at the offer. It's quite attractive, but I've yet to respond to him. I'm still trying to weigh my options. Dad has me working my behind off for a *possible* promotion and Kevin wants to offer me so much more. It would look fantastic on my résumé." She pleaded that last line.

Chris sat back twirling a pen between his thumb and index finger. Several beats elapsed before he spoke again. "It's a start-up. There's no guarantee this company will be around in a year. What happens then?"

Jewel pictured having to ask her father for her old job back. She held her hands up and let them fall in her lap. "I don't know. What I do know is that I want more. I'm ready, but Dad doesn't seem convinced. He's turned me down before. I can't help but feel like I'd have a better chance if I weren't his kid. Maybe my only way up is out.

Kevin seems confident that I am just what his company needs. It's great to feel valued." Jewel looked down at her hands. She'd been wringing them. "Dad always told us not to be afraid to take risks."

"You don't feel valued here, sis?" Chris's head tilted with concern.

Jewel looked away. "Not always."

Chris sighed. Just then his desk phone rang. "That's Dad now." Chris snatched the receiver and placed it against his ear. "Hey, Dad. Yes…" Chris looked at Jewel and mouthed, "Are you hungry?" She shrugged and then nodded. "Yes…that sounds good…okay. We'll be there… okay, bye." Chris turned his attention back to Jewel. "Dad wants us to join him for lunch."

The two of them stood and started toward the door. "Listen." Jewel stopped and swung around to face Chris. "This is between you and me. Got it?"

Chris held his hands up in surrender. "Got it."

Jewel headed to lunch with two things weighing on her mind: the idea of going on an actual date with Sterling and whether or not this COO opportunity would be worth what she would give up to take the position. She wished she could call Sterling to get his opinion on the latter. Jewel shook her head. Here she was wishing she could talk to him. Whether she wanted to admit it or not, he'd already gotten past many of her defenses. Would her standards be the next thing to tumble like a row of dominoes?

Chapter 16

Sterling stood by proudly as Alex led the demonstration of Chandler Food Corp's new software system. The company's top executives were seated around the conference table, including Mrs. Chandler and Jewel's two sisters who worked in other divisions of the empire. With only standing room left, the rest of the employees covered the space from wall to wall watching the presentation describing what their new systems were now capable of doing. The state-of-the-art hardware and software would ensure the company's systems would now run much more efficiently in every area of business.

Keeping his focus mainly on Alex, Sterling's gaze would periodically slide in Jewel's direction. They even locked eyes once or twice. Sterling simply smiled. He'd missed her and their weekly chats in her office, but after the day her father came in unexpectedly, he thought it best to keep his distance. That was a wake-up call for Sterling. Never before had he carried himself so comfortably with a client. That kind of behavior wasn't good for business and he definitely didn't want to cause any issues for Jewel. He knew how bad she'd wanted that promotion. Sterling had to settle for the texts and phone calls. Those interactions weren't as satisfying as seeing her beautiful face, but they had to suffice.

Now that their work was complete and Mr. Chandler had written a stellar recommendation letter, he felt free to pursue Jewel. As soon as their presentation was done, he was going to ask her to dinner. He already had the perfect place in mind.

"And before we take questions, I'd like to call the owners of SB Tech Solutions to the front. Please help me welcome Sterling and Stephan Bishop." Alex nodded and initiated applause.

Sterling was humbled by this elaborate introduction. It wasn't quite necessary for a breakfast presentation. On the other hand, Stephan bowed when he reached the front. Laughter erupted throughout the room.

"You can tell which one of us was the class clown in school," Sterling said. Stephan pretended to secretly point to Sterling and there was more laughter. With hands clasped together, Sterling continued, "I want to thank you—" he tilted his head in Mr. Chandler's direction "—Mr. Bob Chandler for giving our company the great privilege of taking on this project and trusting us. We're glad that you are pleased."

Sterling presented Stephan with a wave of his hand.

"We strive to be the finest in the business and deliver the best in product and customer service. It has been a pleasure working with the entire staff here at Chandler Food Corp." Stephan picked up where Sterling left off.

After a few more words, Mr. Chandler stood. "And we thank you for a fine job. We're excited to be able to do more, faster." He turned to Jewel. "And to my daughter

Jewel. Thank you for all of your hard work in managing this process." He turned his attention to the room of employees. "I'm excited to introduce you to Chandler Food Corp's new vice president of operations."

Sterling watched Jewel's expression turn from momentary confusion, to shock. She stood, looking rather polished in her black business dress and multicolored pumps. To Sterling, Jewel was as sexy as she was professional and he wondered how she managed to pull that off.

Sterling joined in the applause as she made her way to the front of the room and stood beside Mr. Chandler.

"I hope you will do us the honor of signing this offer letter."

Jewel took the paper and hugged her father. "Thank you. Of course I will." She turned to the others in the room. "And thank you all for being such a pleasure to work with." Applause exploded throughout the room once again.

All of the employees cleared out, save the crumbs that had been left from the breakfast. Sterling let Stephan, Alex and the rest of the crew head back to the office without him. He had one more thing to take care of before leaving Chandler Food Corp.

"Congratulations."

Jewel looked up. Her doe eyes gleamed. Her fire-red lips against her fair skin made her look even more radiant.

She smiled and Sterling felt warmth pool in his groin. It had been a long time since a woman had this kind of effect on him.

"Thanks." She nodded humbly. They drank each other in for a moment, maintaining firm eye contact. "I guess this is my last visit, huh?"

Sterling stepped toward her confidently, slowly erasing the distance between them. "It doesn't have to be."

Jewel raised her brow and her lips eased into a wide sly grin. "Really?"

"Yes. Really." Sterling's voice dipped lower.

Jewel eased back against her chair, crossed her legs and folded her arms over her chest. "Okay. Yes."

"Yes what?" He enjoyed the game Jewel was playing. Her coolness made her even more desirable.

"I'll let you take me to dinner." A confident smile played at the corners of her mouth. Sterling almost didn't notice the slight dance on her pretty lips due to the intensity in the way she looked up at him.

Sterling wanted to take her face in his hands and kiss her right then and there. He became sharply aware of his own heartbeat. It thumped at every pulse point.

"Want to name the place and the time, too?" He parked himself on the edge of her desk.

"No." He was amused by the self-assured way she wiggled her head. "I'll leave that up to you."

"What about tonight?"

"Tonight, huh?"

"Yes. Tonight." Sterling stood and headed for the door. "Clear your calendar. I'll pick you up at seven thirty."

The sweet sound of Jewel's laugh followed him out of her office. Seven thirty wouldn't arrive fast enough.

Chapter 17

Jewel tried her best not to act anxious but she couldn't deny the fact that she was excited about her date with Sterling. Her phone rang and she snatched it off the vanity in her dressing room.

"This is Jewel." She answered formally since she hadn't bothered to look and see who was calling.

"You're going, right?"

"Ha! Yes, Dom. I told you and Harper that in the car."

"I know. I just wanted to make sure the fumes from that rush hour traffic didn't affect your mind. You're really going to go out with him?" she asked incredulously. "I'm impressed."

"Yes. Now let me get ready," Jewel said in the same whiny fashion that a teen would say to her mother.

"Okay. What are you wearing?"

"A little black dress. Perfect for any scenario."

"How little?"

"Dom!"

Dominique's laughter poured through the phone. Jewel pictured her friend bent forward, holding her sides.

"Okay. Okay!" She snickered. "Now go have fun with that fine specimen of the male kind and when you get home, call me and Harp to tell us all about it. Okay?"

"After this, I no longer want to hear anything from your and Harper's mouths about my being superficial."

"I'm already zipping my lips. Have fun." Dominique hung up.

Still amused by her friend's behavior, Jewel chuckled to herself as she finished dressing. She looked in the mirror again, standing with one hand planted on her hip and her head cocked to the side. The three dresses she'd tried on so far lay across the white settee in the center of her dressing room and she was still deciding if this fourth one would make the cut. The strapless number, with a ruffle along the top, hugged her curves just right, yet was comfortable enough for her not to feel overdressed. Sterling hadn't mentioned where he was taking her. Looking forward to being surprised, Jewel hadn't asked, which made the decision about what to wear that much more difficult.

Jewel walked over to the wall housing her shoe collection. Taping a finger to her chin, she squinted as she scanned the shelves looking for a perfect pair to complement her outfit. Stilettos would make her appear too dressy. Flats wouldn't be dressy enough. Finally, she settled on a sandal with a low heel that could go either way. Jewel slipped her manicured feet into the strappy sandals and twisted sideways in the mirror. She nodded her head at her reflection, approving of her final choice.

"Now—" Jewel spun on her heel and walked to the other side of the dressing room "—what bag should I carry?" The doorbell rang as she perused the custom-built cubes where her purses were stored. She looked at

"4 for 4" MINI-SURVEY

We are prepared to **REWARD** you with 2 FREE books and 2 FREE gifts for completing our MINI SURVEY!

FREE Value Over $20!

You'll get...

TWO FREE BOOKS & TWO FREE GIFTS

just for participating in our Mini Survey!

Dear Reader,

IT'S A FACT: if you answer 4 quick questions, we'll send you **4 FREE REWARDS!**

I'm not kidding you. As a leading publisher of women's fiction, we value your opinions... and your time. That's why we are prepared to **reward** you handsomely for completing our mini-survey. In fact, we have 4 Free Rewards for you, including 2 free books and 2 free gifts.

As you may have guessed, that's why our mini-survey is called **"4 for 4".** Answer 4 questions and get 4 Free Rewards. It's that simple!

Thank you for participating in our survey,

Pam Powers

www.ReaderService.com

To get your 4 FREE REWARDS:
Complete the survey below and return the insert today to receive 2 FREE BOOKS and 2 FREE GIFTS guaranteed!

"4 for 4" MINI-SURVEY

1 Is reading one of your favorite hobbies?
  ☐ YES   ☐ NO

2 Do you prefer to read instead of watch TV?
  ☐ YES   ☐ NO

3 Do you read newspapers and magazines?
  ☐ YES   ☐ NO

4 Do you enjoy trying new book series with FREE BOOKS?
  ☐ YES   ☐ NO

YES! I have completed the above Mini-Survey. Please send me my 4 FREE REWARDS (worth over $20 retail). I understand that I am under no obligation to buy anything, as explained on the back of this card.

168/368 XDL GMYK

FIRST NAME	LAST NAME

ADDRESS

APT.#	CITY

STATE/PROV.	ZIP/POSTAL CODE

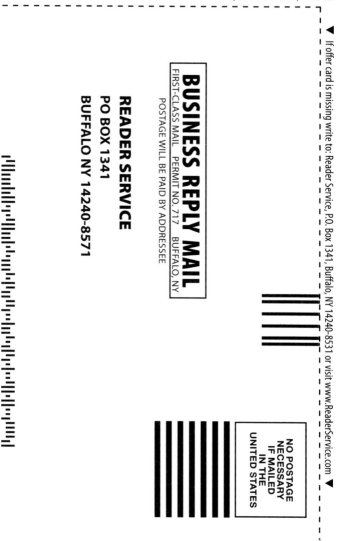

the studded clock on the wall. "Darn it." Seven thirty had slipped by minutes ago. "Coming!"

Jewel raced down the steps, peeked through the blinds and saw Sterling's frame at her door.

"Good evening, Mr. Bishop." Jewel batted her eyes and smiled, turning on her feminine charm or her "girl powers" as her aunt Ava would say.

The wide smile on Sterling's face let her know that he appreciated what he saw.

"Good evening."

"Come on in." Jewel turned, gesturing for him to follow her through the foyer. "I'll need just a few more minutes. Can I get you something in the meantime? Water—a stiff drink. Ha!"

Sterling laughed, too. "I may need one, but I'll start with water." Jewel was aware of his eyes on her as he followed her to the kitchen. "You have a beautiful home. It's just you in this big house by yourself, huh?"

"Just me!" Jewel pulled a bottle of water from the door of the refrigerator and handed Sterling a glass with ice. She picked up a small remote and hit the power button. Music flowed from hidden speakers. "Be right back." Jewel disappeared up the steps.

"I'll be waiting."

At the top of the stairs, Jewel paused, closed her eyes, inhaled and let her breath out slowly. Sterling looked gorgeous in his all–navy blue attire. His look carried the right amount of sex appeal. She shimmied to the bedroom.

Jewel picked a red purse adding a pop of color to her ensemble and outfitted her lips with a similar hue. She waved off the pile of possible dresses lying across the settee. She'd address those later. After a few squirts of her favorite perfume, she took one last look in the mirror and fluffed her hair before heading back downstairs.

"Ready." Jewel popped into the kitchen, startling Sterling just a bit.

"You look amazing." His gaze washed over her from head to toe and back to her head.

"Thank you." A playful smile tugged at the corners of her lips.

Sterling placed his glass in the sink, walked over to her and offered his elbow. Jewel slipped her hand through the opening and together, they walked arm in arm to the car.

"Now where did you say you were taking me?" she asked once they pulled away from her house.

"I didn't say."

"Just checking." She lifted her chin and nestled into her seat.

Sterling laughed and shook his head. "You're a character."

"I know."

"I like it." Sterling winked.

Jewel tittered. Sterling was about to find out just how much of a character she was. As a woman who loved a good time, she didn't hold back and wondered if Sterling could handle her level of zeal. It didn't really matter, she thought, since this would be their only date. With his playful nature, brilliant mind and chart-soaring sex appeal, she knew she'd enjoy his company, but nothing long-term could ever come from their union. She decided that she'd at least like to stay friendly with Sterling. He was easy to talk to and he was good for bouncing ideas off. Jewel was sure they'd make great friends. She'd even flirt with him—often.

"So are you going to give me a hint?" She went back

to trying to get information from him about his plans for the night.

"Yes. We're going to…have a great time."

Jewel swatted his arm. "That's not fair."

"Cheating the other week on the golf course wasn't fair either," Sterling teased.

Jewels mouth dropped open. "I did not cheat!" She turned to face him as he drove. "It was a fair game. You just underestimated me! You should never assume. Ha!"

Sterling's laughter was robust, filling the inside of the car. It was contagious, causing Jewel to join him. She decided she liked the sound if it.

His laugh rolled on while he shook his head at her. They eased into stimulating banter while he drove for the next few minutes before pulling over near a pier by the Long Island Sound. Sterling exited, rounded the car, and opened Jewel's door, helping her to her feet. Keeping her hand in his, he led her along the pier to the dock where a sleek yacht with script letters spelling *Sweet Grace* awaited.

A gentleman expertly suited in captain's attire gave Jewel a courteous smile, tipped his hat with a nod and helped her on the vessel. Sterling followed closely behind. Onboard a slim woman wearing a smart nautical-inspired dress and navy bow tie greeted them with flutes of champagne. Other than these two, they seemed to be the only ones on the boat.

"Oh! I love being on the water." Jewel's hand instinctively went to her chest. "I want to check out the boat." She looked to Sterling.

"Let's do it."

They walked from the cockpit to the deck and up to the flying bridge where the captain sat to steer.

"I haven't steered a boat in years."

"Perhaps after dinner, you can give it a go, madam." The captain looked at Sterling as if he were seeking his approval.

"Cool!" Sterling lifted his brow.

"Wonderful!" Jewel squealed.

Next they went inside the cabin. Jewel fingered the wood grain walls, taking in the traditionally decorated space with burgundy leather sofas and wing chair. Fishing memorabilia hung along the walls. In the center was a table set for two.

"We'll come here if it gets too chilly for you outside."

"That's sweet of you, Sterling. I should be fine. I love watching the water."

The Captain peeked inside. "We're ready to sail." With a nod, he tipped his hat. Sterling nodded back and the captain disappeared.

Jewel wondered where the woman had gone, but abandoned her mental search when she felt Sterling take her hand again. His touch sparked more than just her attention. The tingle surprised her.

"Let's go have dinner."

Their table had been set with a mixed green salad. The candles in the center flickered an amber glow. Jewel still hadn't seen the woman. It seemed almost magical that the food was there. The boat began moving just as she sat down. Sterling took both her hands in his and bowed his head for a quick silent prayer. Jewel was impressed. She closed her eyes and lowered her head as well.

"Bon appétit," Sterling said as he lifted his head. He snapped his napkin and laid it across his lap.

In perfect timing, music began to flow from hidden speakers. Jewel swayed to the rhythm as they talked and ate. The woman appeared to replace their salad plates with an entrée of fish over risotto with chopped asparagus. Jewel moaned at her first bite.

"Sterling, this is absolutely delicious."

"I'm glad you're enjoying it. Wait until dessert. It should be ready in time for the sunset."

"You've thought of everything."

"You try to make all the right moves when you have a beautiful woman to impress."

"So. You're trying to impress me?"

"Maybe." Sterling shrugged like it was no big deal. "Why? Are you impressed?"

"Maybe." She shrugged, then smiled.

The music changed to a popular upbeat song, which happened to be one of Jewel's favorites. She swiped the napkin from her lap and set it on the table.

"My goodness. I love this song. Let's dance."

Immediately, Sterling stood and held out his hand. She placed her hand in his and caught his eye. Sterling winked. They rounded the table and began moving in time together. They danced, song after song until their bodies grew warm and their meal became cold. Jewel didn't mind at all. They were having way too much fun. The song switched to an older song that went along with a popular dance from their teenage years.

"Oh! Remember this?" Sterling laughed.

"Goodness, yes! This was my favorite. What was that dance that went with this?" The two laughed for several moments trying to remember.

"I think I remember." Sterling moved one leg in a circular motion and then shifted into a stance that looked like he was about to take off flying.

Jewel bent back holding her belly, releasing a wild

laugh into the wind. "No! Wait! It went like this." She mimicked similar movements barely finishing her attempt because she was laughing so hard. "Oh my goodness."

They laughed through a few more old dances for the next few songs and the music changed again. A sultry love song shifted the atmosphere. Jewel stood still, suddenly more aware of Sterling's manner of sexiness. Dim evening light settled around him like a halo. His skin glistened from the sheen of sweat they managed to work up. A strong, taut chest peeked through the top of his shirt where a few buttons at the top were left open. He watched her watching him. Jewel swallowed, but kept looking right back into his hazel eyes. She sensed a hunger erupting.

The boat swayed and Jewel fell into his arms. Sterling closed them around her and leaned forward until he was a hair's width from her lips and stopped. Tensions crackled between them. The energy of their closeness tickled her lips. Jewel willed herself not to reach up and kiss him. She could already taste his lips. She imagined they held some of the tartness of the wine they drank. Jewel righted herself in his arms and allowed that closeness to linger for a moment longer.

"Let's go watch the sunset." Sterling's voice was almost a whisper. Leading her by the hand, they grabbed glasses of wine and walked to the deck at the front of the boat. In silence they held hands and watched the sun make a show of its descent. Pink and orange hues turned red and nearly purple before the sun fully tucked itself away.

Sterling led Jewel inside the cabin. They sat at the candlelit table there and enjoyed dessert. Music continued to float through the speakers in a variety of genres. They were back at love songs.

Sterling stood and held his hand out to Jewel. She took it, rose to her feet and stepped into his arms. They swayed to the soothing tempo. Jewel laid her head against his chest. His chest felt as if it were made for her to rest there. When she looked back up at him, Sterling leaned forward and captured her lips with his. When they connected, Jewel wasn't sure if the sway she felt was caused by the boat, or the dizzying effect of Sterling's kiss. He tightened his arms around her. She held him back. He kissed her breath away.

An urgent need came over Jewel and she wondered if Sterling sensed it or felt the same. That need charged them both. Jewel's hands roamed his back and torso and pulled him closer to her. He cupped her bottom, pressing her into him. Sterling released her lips and took to her neck. She arched back, granting him more access. A moan rose in her throat and surprised her. Jewel felt her sense of control slipping away. Placing both hands against his chest, she gently moved back, pushing distance between them. She focused on catching her breath.

"I want to drive the boat." Sterling looked confused. Jewel had to do something to keep herself from going too far. She needed air. "Come on." She took him by the hand and led him up to the flying bridge.

"The lady would like to drive." Sterling alerted the captain.

He simply smiled, stepped aside and waved Jewel over. "Have you ever done this before?"

Jewel giggled. "I have, but it's been a very long time."

The captain offered a quick tutorial and Jewel took the wheel.

"Wooo!" Jewel thrust one fist in the air as she disturbed the quiet of the night sea. Both Sterling and the captain laughed. Jewel enjoyed the wind against her face as she steered for several minutes.

"Now I'm impressed," Sterling said.

For the remainder of the ride, Jewel and Sterling sat on the deck watching the moonlight bounce in the water. The back of her head rested against his chest as they talked about nothing in particular. Jewel couldn't imagine she'd enjoy his company this much. By the time they debarked, she was still fighting her urges for him. They stopped at a bar on the pier and shared another glass of wine before Sterling drove her back home.

When they pulled up to the front of her house, neither of them seemed to want the night to end. She still fought the urge to grab his face and kiss those luscious lips again. They sat together in silence after saying good-night.

"Come inside." Jewel didn't want to fight anymore.

"Are you sure?"

"Completely sure."

They exited his car in haste. Seconds after entering her home they were locked in each other's embrace. Wild kisses and hasty hands unleashed hunger they tried to contain. Jewel backed him against the door, never breaking their kiss. Sterling ran his thumbs over her breasts. Her nipples pebbled. She pushed herself against him, feeling his swell nudge above her pelvic area. Sterling lifted her up. Jewel cradled him with her legs.

"My…my room," she breathed. "Upstairs," Jewel managed past her panting.

Sterling obliged, carrying Jewel upstairs with her legs wrapped around his back. Their lips connecting most of the way. Their kisses, deliciously insistent. In the room, he gently laid her on the bed. She tugged at the buttons on his shirt, trying her best not to snap any off. Sterling pulled down the top of her dress, releasing her mounds. Flicking his tongue against her nipples caused them to harden. He opened wide and took an ample amount in his mouth to suckle. Jewel moaned her delight.

Sterling lifted her dress from the bottom, kissed a trail down her torso, stopping at her navel, and then carrying on to the soft folds of her center. He buried his face there, massaging her to the heights of ecstasy with his skillful tongue. Jewel grabbed handfuls of sheets and screamed his name with her powerful release. His eyes closed and his back arched at her obvious pleasure. They were kindred lovers.

When the trembling waned, she reached for his erection. It was long and firm in her hand. She stroked him gently. The muscles in his taut stomach clenched visibly from her touch. As ready as Sterling was, Jewel sensed that he sought approval.

"Yes." Her voice was just above a whisper. Yearning lived in it.

Sterling reached down into the pockets of the pants dangling around his ankles and pulled out his wallet. He handed the condom to Jewel. She rolled it over his erection. He entered her in the midst of a greedy kiss. Sterling swallowed her moan as he filled her. The fit was snug—perfect. When their lips parted, they stared into each other's eyes as she received his long delectable strokes. Sterling slowed, sped up, just to slow down again. The intensity of their connection threatened to send Jewel to the edge of her own sanity.

Jewel knew exactly when sheer ecstasy descended on him. Sterling moved faster and then faster still. His rhythmic strokes, which she met beat for beat, became erratic. The friction was almost too sweet for Jewel to handle. Sterling's head jerked back. His eyes closed. Jewel tried not to let the immense pleasure take her under. She wanted to fully experience every enchanting second of their jaunt. Jewel could feel the rumble of his groan start in his core, ride his torso and roar through his lips. Their releases collided carrying them on a wave of pure delight, lifting them far beyond their sensibilities. Together they bucked and collapsed into each other. Sterling held her tight. His body seemed too rigid to give.

When her body finally stopped trembling and his muscles relaxed, he planted a sweet series of kisses across her forehead. Jewel had never experienced a more thrilling encounter with any man.

As she lay in Sterling's arms through the night, Jewel determined that she didn't want this to be their one and only time together. From the moment he stepped into her house to pick her up, he'd managed to stimulate every part of her. Sterling had stirred something in her emotionally, mentally, intellectually and now physically. Compatible or not, Jewel wanted more of Sterling Bishop. Of course she wasn't sure how that would work or if it even made sense.

Chapter 18

Sterling looked over at Jewel's beautiful sleeping form and flashes of the past week flickered in his mind's eye. Something intensely magnetic exploded between them when their bodies connected and they had become indivisible. She stimulated his intellect just as much as his loins. In her absence, Sterling craved every part of her, feeling drawn to her by some intangible force. None of his exes had that effect on him. Being with her was indulgent—decadently satisfying to his soul.

Sterling watched her slumber for several moments, appreciating the way her soft mounds rose and fell as she breathed. He reminisced over the time they spent together. Their whirlwind progression made the past week feel more like several weeks. They'd spent every evening together since their first night on the yacht, sharing delectable dinners, enjoying wine tastings, movies and simple nights in, ending many of those days in bed. By the end of the week, she'd spent the night at his place and now he was waking up at hers again. The sex between them was intoxicating and explosive, gripping them like a strong addiction. Leaning over, he kissed her forehead gently.

Jewel stirred, slowly opened her eyes, blinked and smiled. Sterling touched her lip but then moved his finger as if he'd touched fire. What was happening to him? He'd never been one to fall hard and fast for any woman. Organized and calculated—that's what Sterling was. He thought things through and planned them out. That's why he was so successful in business. Somehow with Jewel he'd abandoned his own character. She tapped into a spontaneity he didn't realize existed within him. With the flick of her hair, she challenged his ability to maintain steadfast control of his actions and will.

"Mmm," she moaned.

"Good morning." Sterling leaped from her bed, putting distance between them. Maybe that would help him contain the desire rising in him. He looked down at his growing erection. *Nope.* Distance hadn't helped. He headed for the shower. In just a week, he was as familiar with her home as he was with his.

"Where are you going?" Jewel purred. His erection tensed.

"Shower." He kept walking, hoping to steady his resolve. Everything about her intrigued him: the sweet feminine scent, the sound of her voice; the way her lips easily slid into that sexy smile of hers; the sway of her gait.

"Can I join you?"

Sterling halted, took a deep breath and flung caution to the wind. She was too satisfying to resist and his insatiable desire for Jewel couldn't be doused with a cool shower. "You can join me anytime."

Jewel dipped her chin toward her shoulder and snickered. Sterling chuckled, more at himself for his inability to engage any resistance toward her. Within a few short steps he was at the edge of her bed. He climbed in and held himself over her. His erection bulged in his boxers.

Jewel rose to kiss his nose, turned her head and covered her mouth with her hand. "Morning breath."

Sterling shrugged. Her scent could never be spoiled.

"Move it, silly. I need to brush my teeth before I say another word," she mumbled through tight covered lips.

Sterling groaned, but rolled over anyway.

He stood, took her by the hand and led her to the bathroom. Under the spray of the showerhead, they kissed, devouring each other with urgency like they were satisfying a prolonged hunger. Sterling's hands roamed, squeezed and caressed every part of her body. Her groans were an exotic song, imploring him to keep going.

Sterling lifted Jewel, holding her by her bottom. Jewel wrapped her legs around his back as the water cascaded over them.

"Wait," Jewel whispered breathlessly, bringing Sterling to his senses.

"I'll be right back." Sterling released Jewel slowly until she stood steadily on her feet. He exited the shower, ran to his slacks that had been strewn across the floor the night before and searched for protection. Pulling it from his pocket, he held it up like a prize and rejoined Jewel in the shower.

"Now where were we?" He donned a slick grin.

Jewel snickered, took the condom from his fingers and their lips connected as she tore open the package and rolled it onto his erection. Without breaking the kiss, he lifted her in his arms again. Jewel wrapped her legs around his back. She hissed as Sterling slid inside of her. Instinctively his body responded to their perfect fit. Sterling's eyes closed and his head fell back. Jewel's moans strung together creating an erotic melody. The song invaded Sterling's core. The tempo of his rhythm increased. They slammed into each other faster and faster, reaching a quick peak, then melted against one another. The clear shower doors clouded from the steam they created.

Sterling washed Jewel and she returned the favor. He fought the urge to be inside of her once again. Not wanting to leave, he prolonged getting dressed. The rest of his day was open and he wouldn't mind spending it with Jewel. Overstaying his welcome was the last thing he wanted to do. He was known for pacing himself.

As if reading his thoughts, Jewel suggested they go for breakfast together. That breakfast led to them spending the rest of the day in each other's presence and a stroll along the pier with ice cream while they watched the sunset. No topic escaped them, whether political, professional or personal. Sterling found Jewel so easy to talk to. Their conversations weren't plagued with sharp pauses because of opposing views like it had been with his ex-wife. Instead, any opinionated opposition was met with lively debates and respectful but playful banter.

The night found them back at her place, with their bodies comfortably folded on the sofa in her family room. Music settled in the background. Conversation continued to flow effortlessly as if they'd never run out of things to talk about. Even the momentary bouts of silence that fell between them were comfortable and well placed.

Jewel shifted her position on the sofa and turned to study Sterling for a moment. "Why didn't things work out between you and your ex-wife?"

Sterling sat back and breathed for a moment before answering.

"I'm sorry. I didn't mean to be intrusive," Jewel said, misinterpreting his silence.

"Don't be. I was just thinking about where to start."

Jewel shrugged. "I was just curious. That's all. I remember you saying it didn't last a year. That's rather short." She paused. "You don't have to answer that." She dismissed her inquiry with a wave of her hand. "Sorry," she said again.

"I don't mind. We dated for a while, but I'm not sure either of us really wanted to be married. I felt obligated because she was pregnant. When she told me, we just moved fast—eloped and found an apartment and then a house. We figured it was the best thing to do. At first it was cool but it didn't take long to go sour. She had the baby and while we loved our daughter, we only tolerated each other. I think we expected that love would extend to us, but it never did."

"Oh."

"We tried to salvage the marriage—went to a therapist for a few sessions. Nothing much came of that. One day I asked myself, 'Would I be happier with or without her?' When I couldn't definitely answer that question I knew it was time for a change. I asked her the same thing. It didn't seem to matter to her either way. Our relationship was over before it started. All we had between us were the best intentions." Sterling thought for a moment. The fact that he never regretted their breakup was his constant confirmation that they had done the right thing. "I believe that we should marry the person that we couldn't possibly see ourselves living without."

Jewel smiled. "That's sweet." She paused. "And it makes a lot of sense."

"Yeah."

"Would you ever marry again?"

"Absolutely. When I find that woman that I can't see myself living without."

"That's special." Jewel looked down and fiddled with her fingers.

To Sterling, it seemed she'd grown uncomfortable with the subject, but she had been the one to bring it up.

"What about you? Do you see yourself ever getting married?"

"Yeah. I'm not in a rush. I think it's important to take time to find someone with whom you're equally yoked."

"Interesting. And what does *equally yoked* mean for you?" Sterling curled his fingers into quotes.

"Well." Jewel sighed. "Sharing a certain…common ground. Being compatible in specific ways. Having similar goals."

"Uh-huh." Sterling nodded as he studied her.

Jewel looked at him skeptically at first and then shrugged. "It doesn't really matter. My husband is probably far off in the future anyway. Most people seem to think I have an odd way of determining compatibility." She cleared her throat, reached for the empty wine glasses and stood. "Can I get you something more to drink?"

Sterling recognized her actions as the end of their discussion. He wasn't going to push her. He took the glasses from her and placed them back on the table. With her face cupped between both hands, he pulled her toward him for a sensual kiss. He felt her body melt under the intensity and heat. His groin awakened once again. Sterling pressed himself against her. After a moment he pulled away. As much as he wanted to stay another night, it was time to go.

Sterling held her, resting his hands against her bottom. "I gotta get going." His voice came out as a whisper. Jewel panted with her head on his chest. Her pulse had quickened. Sterling could feel it thumping.

"Okay," Jewel whined and grinned. "I enjoyed your company."

"I enjoyed your hospitality." Sterling raised his brows two quick times and both of them laughed knowing *company* and *hospitality* sounded much lighter than the explosiveness that really transpired between them.

Reluctance changed the air around them. Jewel trudged toward the door behind him. Sterling didn't really want to go either, but he had to prepare for his daughter's arrival. He was going to mention the real reason he needed to leave but chose to keep that bit of information to himself.

Jewel would meet Kylee—and soon. With the way he was feeling about Jewel, their meeting was not only inevitable but necessary. With Kylee's approval, he'd feel comfortable and unhindered in his pursuit of Jewel because he already knew he wanted her.

Chapter 19

Dominique shuffled into the restaurant like a gust of wind snatching both Harper and Jewel's attention at the same time. Jewel sipped her wine, laughed and shook her head.

"Weren't you the one who told me not to be late?" Jewel raised a brow at Dominique.

"I know. I know." Dominique plopped her purse on the table and flopped into her seat. "Oh my goodness. What a day!"

"Sounds like all of us had interesting days." Harper sighed.

"Sorry for being late. What are we drinking?"

Jewel raised her glass. "Cabernet Sauvignon."

"Pinot." Harper pointed at her drink.

Dominique raised her hand signaling the waiter who hurried over. She ordered Jewel's drink and turned back to the ladies. "What did I miss?"

"Nothing. Of course we were going to wait until the circle was complete before spilling all the juice."

"I know. Let's order and get started. Work has been so crazy I feel out of touch with every area in my life."

"Me, too," Harper said. "Besides the fact my boss tried to make a pass at me."

"What!" Dominique and Jewel barked together.

"Okay. You start! What happened?" Jewel asked.

"He's the cute new one, right?" Dominique seemed excited. "Was he a jerk about it?" she asked.

"Or did you actually like it?" Jewel asked, raising a brow. "You don't seem upset."

"Whoa! One at a time." Harper held her hands up. "It was actually sweet."

"Sweet!" Dominique reared back.

"What does that mean?" Jewel sipped.

The waiter checked in and they ordered meals.

"First he complimented my dress and immediately apologized. I said thanks and told him no apology was needed. Then he sighed like something was wrong. I asked if he was okay and he said this…" She paused. Jewel and Dominique leaned in. Harper giggled. "'I didn't want to offend you. It's just that you really are beautiful and I was trying to find a way to say that without being inappropriate. I hope that doesn't make you uncomfortable.'"

"Aww. That is kind of sweet, isn't it Jewel."

"It depends on what happens next. What day was this?"

"Monday."

"How has he been since then?" Jewel asked.

"Almost like a shy kid with a crush. He avoids being around me unless there's a business need, but he has checked in a time or two to make sure I was comfortable but it's clear that he has a thing for me."

"Wow! That certainly makes for an interesting work environment," Dominique said.

"Do you feel comfortable? Because that's what's important."

"Actually, Jewel, it didn't bother me at all. He wasn't creepy about it and has gone out of his way to make sure it doesn't get creepy."

"Would you date him?" Dominique inquired.

"If he wasn't my boss? Absolutely. He's *gorgeous*!" Harper rolled her eyes.

"Dammit! He needs to get fired!" Jewel slammed her napkin on the table.

Laughter poured from each of them.

"That's all I've got," Harper said once they recovered.

"I think I need to go last. What's happening with you Dom?"

"They're trying to kill me at work. I've been pulling ten-hour shifts. It's been affecting my beauty sleep. And I know I said I'd never date any more attorneys, but I met this guy at one of my company's receptions and he was *G O R G E O U S*. Luckily, I found out that he was a judge so that makes it okay."

"You're going to date him?" Harper asked.

"I don't know. We exchanged cards. He emailed me suggesting we do lunch, but I'm going to wait and see what I find about him first. Did I mention that he was gorgeous?"

"I'd say you pretty much spelled it out for us." Jewel lifted her glass but ended up laughing too hard to take a sip.

"Oh my goodness!" Harper wiped a tear. "This is why I love when we're together. You ladies crack me up. Whew! Okay, Jewel. Your turn."

"Yes. What's up with Sterling Bishop? How was the date? Spill every drop of that scrumptious juice. Don't leave out a single detail!" Dominique ordered.

Jewel grinned, trying to hold the laugh bubbling behind her lips. Both friends sat on the edge of their chairs waiting for her speak. "That date pretty much lasted all week."

"What!" Dominique's voice cracked and carried far beyond their table. Several patrons looked in their direction. The three of them snickered.

"How did this happen?" Harper asked.

"The date was great! We had dinner on a private yacht and went back to my place."

"And." Dominique stretched the short word into several syllables.

Jewel fell back in her seat and laid the back of her hand on her forehead. "It was explosive!"

"Whoa!" Dominique shouted, garnering more stares.

"Wait! What was explosive?"

Jewel and Dominique looked at Harper sideways.

"Oh!" Harper's hand flew to her mouth. Her eyes stretched wide. "Jewel," she sang.

"We hung out for the rest of the week going to the movies, dinner, all kinds of stuff. It was really fun."

"See. I told you to give him a chance. You and this compatibility thing."

Jewel sat straight, holding up a finger. "We had a great time this week, but that doesn't mean this will be anything permanent. I'm having fun while it lasts."

Dominique threw her hands up and let them fall against the table with a slap. "Really, Jewel." She leaned back so the waiter could place their meals on the table. When he walked away, Dominique continued. "Don't lead him on if you really don't want him. He doesn't seem like a player that would take that lightly."

Jewel twisted her lips. "I'm not leading the man on. It's only been a week. It's not that serious."

"What if it gets serious?" Harper asked, taking in a mouthful of pasta.

"It won't. I won't let it. He has an ex-wife and a child, remember?"

Dominique waved her comment off. "Sometimes serious sneaks up on us."

Jewel shifted in her seat wondering if the girls noticed.

"Let's go back to the juicy details." Harper saved her. "Tell us about the dates."

They enjoyed dinner as Jewel relayed the details of her whirlwind week with Sterling.

"Oh. And Kevin upped his offer. He really wants me to take the position at his company."

"Are you considering it?" Dominique's fork only made it halfway between her plate and her mouth.

"Didn't your dad give you the promotion?" Harper asked.

Jewel looked toward Harper first. "Yes. I got the VP position." She directed her attention to Dominique. "The offer is attractive and would give me full reign over operations and would look amazing on my résumé. But I'm not sure if it's the right move. Ugh."

"That's tough." Dominique shook her head.

"When does he want an answer?"

Jewel cut her eyes upward and brought them back down to Harper's line of sight. "Like…yesterday. I've been putting him off and the longer I put him off, the more he sweetens the deal. It isn't about the money. It's about the opportunity. Here's the thing…" Jewel shifted in her seat. "Although I would have a better title at his company, my family's business is actually a better look for my résumé and there's more room for growth. I'm leaning toward staying now that I got the new position. I'm just not sure going to Kevin's company would be worth it."

"You'll have to think that through long and hard." Harper sighed.

"You're right, you need to determine if it will be worth it. I wonder what your dad would make of it. Does he know about it?"

"No!" Jewel shook her head vigorously. "When Sterling and I talked about it this week, he said the same thing."

Dominique dropped her fork. "Really." She looked at Harper and the two of them snickered.

"What?" Jewel looked back and forth between them.

"You're asking Sterling for advice now?"

"Oh please." Jewel waved away their concerns. "Like I said, I'm having fun now but in the end, he'll never be more than a friend."

Dominique narrowed her eyes at Jewel. She didn't seem convinced.

Jewel's phone vibrated. There was a text from her sister for everyone to meet at their mother's house by eight thirty. The display on the phone told her it was past seven thirty.

"Looks like someone called a family meeting tonight. I'm going to have to cut my dinner short, ladies. Sorry."

Harper wiped her mouth with her napkin. "I hope everything is okay."

"Yes, Jewel. Keep us posted."

"Will do."

Jewel quickly finished her meal, said goodbye and headed to her parents' home.

Alarmed by the nondescript text, she pushed the speed past the limits to arrive in record time. Jade and Chris were in the kitchen with their parents. Jewel was even more surprised to see her grandparents, Mary Kate and Freddie.

"Hey Grandma! Hi Granddad." Jewel leaned in for a kiss and Mary Kate squeezed her in a warm embrace.

"How's my favorite baby girl?"

Jewel shimmied into her grandfather's arms.

"Granddad! You just said I was your favorite," Jade scolded him.

"I did, didn't I?" In his usual way, Freddie tittered and sat down, giving neither the satisfaction of a response. His tease made everyone laugh. Mary Kate winked and patted his hand.

"Hey Mom. Hey Dad." Jewel kissed each of them, giving her mother the thumbs-up for her chic pantsuit. El blushed. Jewel then greeted her brother and sister with a hug.

"Where's Chloe?"

"We're waiting for her now." El sat down at the table with her in-laws and a cup of tea.

"Everything okay?" Jewel looked around curiously.

"I guess we'll find out when Chloe gets here. She called the meeting," El said.

"Oh. I thought you and dad called the meeting." Jewel walked to the refrigerator, retrieved a container of orange juice and poured a glass.

The garage door opened and Chloe walked in with Donovan on her heels.

"Hey everyone!" Chloe kissed her grandparents, parents and then her siblings. Donovan greeted the women with hugs and kisses and the men with firm shakes.

"Anybody hungry?"

Chris stood. "Yep."

"You just ate!" Jade admonished.

"Now I want some of my mother's good food." Chris grabbed a dish and handed it to his mother.

Bobby Dale chuckled. El smiled as she piled food onto her son's plate.

"Anyone else?" El asked. Her meals were hard to resist. Everyone but Jewel ate. Instead, she took sample bites from her siblings' plates.

After the meal and a bit of light discussion, Chloe stood and called Donovan up to stand by her side.

Chloe wore an expression mixed with worry and excitement. Jewel wondered what she was about to share with the family. Donovan laced his fingers between hers and placed his other hand gently on her back. His supportive gesture seemed to calm her a bit. Was she pregnant? El would be upset if she had a baby before getting married. Appearances mattered to her.

"What's going on?" Jewel couldn't stand the suspense.

"Donovan and I have set a wedding date."

"Congratulations," Mary Kate and Freddie said together.

"You certainly have our blessing," Bobby Dale said. El nodded with her hand on his shoulder. They were in agreement. "When?"

Donovan looked into Chloe's eyes. "Labor Day weekend."

"Okay." Jade sang the word. "That's a little over two months away. We've got a lot of work to do in a short period of time."

"Yeah. The date is sooner than expected, but I thought you had a real surprise for us," Chris teased.

That couldn't have been the news, Jewel thought. Surely Chloe and Donovan had to know that the family expected they would choose a date soon. There had to be more. Jewel wondered what it was.

"In Puerto Rico," Chloe said in a rush as if she couldn't wait to get the words out of her mouth.

The room fell silent. All eyes went to El. She sat straighter but didn't speak. Ever since Chloe and Donovan's engagement, El had been looking forward to hosting their wedding right at Chandlers. She couldn't wait to make it the biggest event their friends could ever witness and talked about it all of the time. This was good news for everyone except El. This was also another example of Chloe standing her ground and for that she made Jewel proud.

El cleared her throat and set her chin slightly higher. "Well if that's what you want."

"It is what we want, Mom." Chloe's hopeful expression pleaded with El. "The wedding will be held at Donovan's resort." Chloe turned to Donovan. When she looked into his eyes, Jewel swore Chloe's eyes glazed with admiration. Her sister's love for Donovan seeped into the atmosphere.

"I think it's perfect. That's where it all started. Why not get married there?" Jewel said.

"Yes!" Jade chimed in. "How romantic."

"Serenity will love this." Chris walked over to Donovan and shook his hand. "You better take care of my big sister."

"For sure." Donovan patted Chris's arm.

"Well, sweetie," Freddie said to Mary Kate. "I guess we're going to Puerto Rico."

"Good. I can finally wear that two-piece I've been holding on to."

"Uh. Grandma! No two-pieces allowed. Not in Puerto Rico. Not anywhere!" Jade scrunched her nose.

Everyone laughed except El.

"I'm happy to help any way I can." Bobby Dale confirmed his acceptance even as he placed a comforting hand over El's.

"I won't say I'm not disappointed. Chandlers would have been an ideal location for the wedding and everyone would be able to make it."

Everyone waited for Chloe's response. "I'm sure you're disappointed. Mrs. Rivers would have loved to host our wedding at their place as well, but Donovan and I decided that Puerto Rico would be best. It means so much to us."

"Fine." El sat. It was obvious that she wasn't as excited as the rest of the family.

"It would be great to know that we still have your blessing," Donovan said.

El huffed. After a few moments of silence, she nodded.

Jewel noticed Chloe hold Donovan's hand tighter. She looked over at her parents and her father was still holding her mother's hand. The gesture warmed her heart and she found herself wondering what it must be like to have a partner so supporting and comforting. She watched the way both Chloe and her mother appeared calmer. Those simple wordless gestures seemed to mean so much. Jewel hadn't experienced that in a date before. Could she have that with Sterling? Would he be interested in joining her at the wedding? Would she want a destination wedding for herself?

Those random thoughts jolted Jewel. What was she thinking? Her tryst with Sterling could only be temporary. They were having fun but nothing serious could ever come from it—or could it?

Chapter 20

The weeks whizzed by and Sterling had Jewel at his side all along the way. Work, Jewel, family—that was how he'd spent his days. There weren't many places they hadn't gone to together. He'd even done things with Jewel that he'd never done with other women like go shopping. Sterling couldn't believe he had let her coax him into a trip to the mall. He even stood outside of the fitting room giving her the thumbs-up on the outfits she tried on. As far as he was concerned, everything looked amazing on her. Somehow they found themselves in each other's beds on Friday and Saturday nights.

Jewel was a breath of cool spring air. Refreshing, funny, witty, smart and beautiful—she was the complete package. Not to mention she was the first woman to make his toes curl while making love. What more could he ask for? They hadn't defined what they were. She even referred to them as friends, but Sterling wanted more. He couldn't let Jewel get away. He just had to convince her having an ex-wife and daughter would never hinder him from being the man she needed.

Sterling could tell she'd taken issue with these things by the way she withdrew at times when he talked about Kylee. She tried to be discreet, but he always noticed. With starry eyes, she talked about the future and Jewel never mentioned a stepchild in the life she envisioned. That was his only obstacle. Although Jewel appeared to be the perfect woman, there was no way he could move forward with her if she couldn't accept his daughter. Kylee was his world. She had to love Jewel and Jewel would have to love her back. He just needed to show Jewel that it was possible.

Sterling heard his name. Jewel's voice had a way of causing jolts of electricity to course through his body. Everything about her was stimulating.

"What's up, babe?" He'd taken to calling her that in recent weeks.

Jewel trotted down the steps in a tank, ripped jeans and glittery sandals. Her designer handbag hung from her forearm. With her hair pulled back, every exquisite feature in her beautiful face was on full display. Her red sexy lips made his member twitch.

Jewel plopped the purse on the counter, embraced Sterling and wrapped her feet around his back. As Sterling laughed, he had to steady himself to avoid letting her slip. Jewel threw her head back and laughed, too, releasing music into the air and drowning out the sound of the bacon sizzling in the pan. She kissed him all over his face before sliding back to her feet.

Sterling kept her in his arms and kissed her forehead. Air circulated in his chest. Her playful nature really did something inexplicable to him.

"I've gotta go. Our dresses for the wedding came in and we need to get fitted." Jewel grabbed a mini croissant, tore it open and laid two slices of bacon inside. "You won't believe how much we managed to get done in a few short weeks." She took a bite. "I can't believe the big day is less than two months away."

Mention of the wedding made Sterling imagine Jewel's beautiful body under a tropical sun. The thought made him desire her right then and there. "You're coming back tonight, right?"

Jewel sauntered toward him—her head cocked sideways and her lips pouted. Placing a hand on his cheek, she whispered, "Want me to?"

"Ha!" Sterling looked at the ceiling and mentally counted down from ten. It didn't work. A slight erection worked in his jeans. "You better leave. Now!"

Jewel giggled, rose to her toes and planted another kiss on his lips. Grabbing her purse she trotted to the door. "See you later."

"Kylee's looking forward to meeting you," he called after her. The door shut.

Sterling closed his eyes and took a deep breath. He wasn't sure if she'd heard him. He couldn't focus on that now. The bacon wasn't going to fry itself and Kylee and Raven's flight would be arriving within the hour.

Seconds later, his phone rang. "Hello."

"I heard you."

Sterling stopped breathing for a quick moment. He didn't speak. The silence expanded and felt constricting.

"I just don't know if it's a good idea to meet your daughter. I mean…are you sure you want her to meet me? You always talk about being careful of who you bring around her. What if she doesn't like me? It's just that—"

"I want you to meet her."

Silence descended on the conversation again. Several beats ticked by without either of them speaking.

"We should talk about this in person." Sterling hoped he didn't sound as dejected as he felt. He knew this wasn't easy for her and understood.

"I know."

"Tonight…after dinner." It was more of a question. Sterling wondered if she was going to show up.

"Okay."

"See you later?"

"See you later."

Sterling ended the call and stood still, gnawing his bottom lip for several moments. In complete silence, he finished preparing his breakfast and then headed to the airport. Though he didn't speak, his mind was a frenzy of hopes and doubts the entire way. Of course they would love each other. Jewel was an amazing woman and Kylee was a sweet girl. If they didn't, he'd have to let Jewel go. She'd already gotten deep inside of him. Letting her go would be like tearing away a piece of himself. How had that happened so soon?

Chapter 21

Jewel sat in front of the restaurant for at least ten minutes before willing herself to step out of the car. She'd explored all the reasons she should leave and drive straight home. What sense did it make to meet this little girl when she had no intentions of staying with Sterling. Yet, she was there.

For some reason, walking away didn't seem as easy as she'd imagined. Outside of his daughter and ex-wife, Sterling was the perfect man. When they were together, she had a blast. He wasn't intimidated by her family's legacy. In fact, he seemed not to be affected by it at all. The other men she dated were either in awe of it or tried unsuccessfully to not appear fazed. Others made her feel as though they were in some kind of competition with regard to their pedigrees. Sterling was Sterling, not his family's accomplishments. And Jewel was just able to be Jewel—for the first time ever.

Another five minutes passed. Jewel pushed the door open and hopped out. She had to at least show up. Curiosity fueled the rest of her determination. The last thing she wanted to do was walk away with regrets. Having dinner with Sterling and his daughter could confirm several things for her. As much as she enjoyed his company, his mind and his…body, she just knew this couldn't work. Going inside would allow her to prove that to both her and Sterling. Then, she would end what they had—have the "we should just be friends" talk with Sterling and move on with her life.

Jewel spotted Sterling the moment she walked up to the host station. Sterling waved and she pointed him out to the hostess. The short walk over to the table seemed to last forever. Sterling stood to greet her, kissing her lips. Jewel tensed and her eyes landed on the cutest girl with a mess of curls springing out of a ponytail.

"Jewel, this is my little princess, Kylee," Sterling pulled out a chair for Jewel. "Kylee, this is Ms. Jewel—daddy's friend." He presented Jewel like a prize as she sat down.

"Daddy," Kylee sang, rolling her eyes. "I know she's your girlfriend. Hi, Ms. Jewel." Kylee held her hand out for Jewel to shake it.

Impressed, Jewel smiled and raised her brows. "It's a pleasure to meet you, Miss Kylee." They shook hands.

"Miss?" she repeated with a pout. "I'm not a grown up."

Sterling and Jewel laughed this time.

"You can still be Miss." Jewel noticed her voice become lighter—playful even.

"I can?" She seemed to be in wonder. "I like that," Kylee declared with a firm nod.

"Me, too!" Jewel matched Kylee's nod.

"You're pretty, Ms. Jewel." Kylee unleashed a smile

so wide, her eyes nearly shut. The adorable grin revealed spaces where two teeth used to be.

Jewel couldn't help but laugh and be softened by Kylee's cuteness. She felt her defenses dissipate just a little. "You're pretty, too, Miss Kylee. Very pretty."

"Thank you!"

The rest of the dinner went as smoothly as it started. Jewel forgot that she was supposed to assess the situation. Instead, she was pulled in by Kylee's charm and really enjoyed her and Sterling's company.

The three of them headed back to a local creamery for ice cream before ending the evening at Sterling's place. The second they hit the door Kylee took Jewel by the hand and raced upstairs to show off her bedroom. As many times as Jewel had been at Sterling's home, this was the first time she saw inside of Kylee's room. She expected pink and frills and instead walked into a whimsical royal blue and purple paradise fit for a trendy princess. The walls alternated in light blue and lavender. A crystal chandelier hung from the center, shining perfect light on large painted letters spelling Kylee's name across one wall and a tiara on the other.

Kylee flopped on the bed and patted the space beside her. "Come sit, Ms. Jewel."

"Okay." Jewel joined her.

"Let's play a game." Kylee pulled out her phone and they took turns driving in the racing game. Kylee twisted and turned her entire body as she navigated the sharp road and explained the rules to Jewel.

When it was Jewel's turn, Kylee fell back cackling each time Jewel crashed the car into a wall, divider or another car.

"It sounds like fun is going on in here." Sterling stood in the doorway.

"I'm a horrible driver." Jewel threw her hands up. "Who knew?"

Kylee's toothless giggle made Jewel laugh harder.

"I hate to be the one to break up all the fun, but it's way past your bedtime."

"Aw, Daddy!" Kylee's gleeful grin was immediately replaced by a sad frown.

Jewel looked at her phone. She couldn't believe it was past ten. She stood.

"I know. Say good-night to Ms. Jewel and go take your shower. When you're all done, I'll tuck you in."

"Okay," she whined as she slid off the bed. "It was nice to meet you, Ms. Jewel." Before Jewel knew it, Kylee had wrapped her arms around her waist.

Jewel felt more of her resolve dissipate. She hesitated for a brief moment before hugging Kylee back. "It was great meeting you, too, Miss Kylee."

Sterling came over and took Kylee by the hand. Kylee looked up, setting her large doe eyes on Jewel. Her heart softened a tad more.

"Daddy is taking me to the movies tomorrow. Can you come with us?" She turned to her father. "Daddy, can she come? Please. Can she?"

Sterling shrugged. "If she wants to."

"Will you come?"

"Sure. I'll come." Jewel's smile was instinctive. That little girl was working her way through her resolve just like her dad had. "Just tell me what time."

"Yay!" Kylee jumped up and down. "See you tomorrow." She hugged Jewel's waist harder this time, knocking her back a step.

Sterling shook his head. "Okay. Time for bed."

"Okay, Daddy!" Sterling received no opposition this time. Kylee was happy.

Sterling turned to Jewel. "Meet you downstairs in a few?"

"Sure."

Jewel headed down to the kitchen and grabbed a bottle of water. She opened it, sipped and exhaled. This dinner was supposed to prove to both of them that moving forward together would never work. That's why she'd held such trepidation at the thought of meeting Sterling's daughter. Now Jewel wasn't so sure of that or anything anymore.

Chapter 22

Sterling couldn't help but sing along with the upbeat song flowing from his Bluetooth speaker. He moved around his bedroom to the beat. His plan had worked. Kylee and Jewel were smitten with each other. Not only did Jewel join them for the movie the next day but they hung out several more times since then. He looked forward to having Kylee closer to home now that Raven was finally done with her master's program. She'd postponed her graduate studies to care for Kylee and then went back when Kylee was a little older. Everything was working out for the best in his life.

Now that he had dropped Kylee and his mother off at the airport, he had the opportunity to spend more adult-only time with Jewel while Kylee was away. He planned the perfect night with the intent to make his intentions crystal clear. Sterling would have both his daughter and the woman who was quickly capturing his heart close by.

Sterling danced around his bed toward the ringing phone on the nightstand. "Hello."

"Hey, Sterling."

"Our baby is on her way to California as we speak. I just got back from dropping her and my mom off at the airport," he said, as he tossed a tank top and pair of shorts on the bed.

"Good...um...are you home right now?"

"Yeah." He began changing out of his jeans and shirt.

"Are you going anywhere?"

"Not until later. What's up?"

"I wanted to stop by. I need to talk to you."

Sterling stopped moving. "Is everything okay?"

"I'll be right there." Raven hung up. He looked at his phone.

Sterling pulled his shorts on, stuffed his feet into sandals and went down to the kitchen. He pulled a cold beer from the refrigerator, stepped onto his back porch and lay back on one of his wicker lounge chairs. He stayed there until he heard the doorbell ring. He dialed Raven's cell number and told her to come around to the back.

"Hey. What's up?" He stood and greeted her with a friendly kiss. "Have a seat. Want a beer?"

"No thanks." Raven took a breath before she sat.

Sterling faced Raven. "Talk to me."

Raven averted her eyes, tucked her lower lip inside her mouth and sighed. Sterling tried not to worry. Whatever she had to say was obviously difficult so he didn't want to rush her but his patience was wearing.

"I got into my PhD program."

That's all she had to say? Sterling was relieved. "That's fantastic, but I knew that already."

"In Chicago."

"What!" Sterling's back straightened. "What happened to the program here in New York—at Hudson?" Sterling pointed, gesturing in the direction of the university.

"The school in Chicago is offering me a full scholarship. It's a stellar program. I can't pass this up."

Sterling put down his beer and stood. Too upset to look directly at Raven, he planted his hands on his hips and looked out into the yard. Grunting, he swiped his palm down his face.

"What does this mean, Raven?" He still hadn't looked her way.

"Kylee and I aren't here to stay. We're heading back at the end of the summer."

"How long did you know this, Raven?" He said her name hard. He felt his eyes boring into her.

"Sterling…"

"How long?" he barked, interrupting her.

Raven lowered her head and groaned. "Since May."

Wide-eyed, Sterling looked at his watch as if he could chart the passage of months there. "It's July!" Sterling palmed his temples, put his hands back on his hips and let them slip off. He stepped sideways and turned around. In his attempts to contain the angry energy coursing through his veins, he didn't know what to do with his body. "I can't believe this." His hands were back on his hips. "I'll pay for the program here in New York."

"I can't let you do that."

"I want my daughter here. That's what we planned." Sterling sat, making the lounge chair tilt and steady itself. "You said three years was all you needed. Our family is here."

"Sterling, please." Raven held her hands up. "This is difficult enough, but I can't let this opportunity pass me by. My sister is still there and can help out with Kylee if I need her to. It's just for a few more years."

Sterling groaned. "Just!"

"Kylee can still spend her summers, school breaks and holidays here with you."

Sterling was on his feet. "I never agreed to being a part-time dad. Just let Kylee live with me."

Now Raven stood. "I'm not giving up my daughter."

"But I have to?" Sterling challenged her with knitted brows.

Raven huffed. "She's a girl. She needs her mother."

"And not her father." Sterling wasn't letting up.

"I'm sorry. This is how it has to be. In a few years it will be all over."

"So now you make all of the decisions for *our* daughter yourself?"

"Sterling…" Raven closed her eyes and shook her head.

All he could do was stare at Raven. If he was less macho, he would have been bawling by now. The way he looked at it, Raven was taking his daughter away from him. For so long, he waited for her to be in the same state—the same community. Now things were changing and there didn't seem to be much he could do about it.

The doorbell rang, startling both of them. Sterling trotted through the house, opened the door and Jewel stepped right in.

"Hey, babe." She stood on her toes and kissed his lips. "I was at the mall and saw the cutest hair clips for Kylee. You know the studded ones she loves." Jewel rifled through the bags. "I got a little something for you, too. Maybe you can wear it tonight." She looked up and the smile melted from her face. She looked at Raven and then back at Sterling.

That's when Sterling realized that Raven had followed him.

"Uh. Hi." Jewel held her hand out. "I'm Jewel."

"Raven, this is my girlfriend, Jewel." Sterling noticed Jewel stand more erect. He knew they hadn't defined what was between then, but he didn't want to leave any room for misunderstandings.

"Hi." Raven shook Jewel's extended hand.

"Is this a bad time?" Jewel asked.

Sterling hated the awkwardness of the encounter.

"Oh. Um. No. I was just leaving." Raven nodded toward Jewel and said, "Nice to meet you," although she didn't sound convincing.

Raven stepped around them and walked out. Jewel looked at the door and then Sterling. "I'm sorry about showing up without calling first."

"You don't need to call." Sterling pulled Jewel in for a kiss. He needed to feel her lips against his. Her touch calmed him. She'd become his balm.

"Are you okay?" Jewel asked once she caught her breath.

Sterling forced a smile and peeked into the bag she was holding. "What do you have for me in here?"

Jewel eyed him suspiciously for several seconds before pulling out a blue shirt. "It reminded me of you."

Despite the plans he had made, Sterling needed to let Jewel know how he felt right in that moment. Taking the bags from her, he took her by the hand and led her to the backyard.

"Sit." Sterling took a seat across from her and held both her hands in his.

"I was saving this for tonight but I think this is the best time." Curiosity seemed to knit Jewel's brows. Sterling smiled because what he was about to say restored the joy he felt before Raven's daunting news. "I don't know what you did to me, but I can't imagine not having you in my life." Jewel's mouth opened. "We haven't defined what we've been doing, but I know I want more of you. I've felt this way for a while, but I had to know that you would accept my daughter and that she would accept you. You were worried about meeting Kylee, but I knew what I was doing. I want to be with you, Jewel. You're not like any other woman I've dated. I've heard you talk about what you want out of life and I know it didn't include a man with a daughter and an ex-wife but I need you to know, you have a place in my life, too, and you'll never be in competition with either of them."

Jewel's mouth opened and closed. She sat blinking at Sterling and finally exhaled.

"You don't need to respond. Just think about what I said. Can you do that for me?"

Jewel pursed her lips. "I have to be honest with you. I never saw myself being in a relationship with someone who had an ex-wife *and* a child. I've always imagined my first child and wedding would also be my partner's first. In fact, until you came along, I was dead set against dating divorcees or men with children. It always seemed to lead to complicated circumstances."

"I figured that. Which is why it was important for me to introduce you to my daughter. You're still here. That's a good sign and I realize that. I believe we have something special and I want to explore it. You're an amazing woman. I'm not willing to let you go without at least trying to see what this can become. So if you'll have me, I'll show you that being a divorced man won't matter at all. I'm very careful about the decisions I make and believe me I've thought about this one thoroughly."

Jewel nodded. Sterling caressed her chin and pulled her to him. He kissed her lips, wrapped his arms around hers and pulled her in for a more passionate exchange. He kissed her with a new intensity causing his desire for her to burgeon even more. Sterling had to stop himself before he ended up carrying her upstairs to the bedroom.

"I've planned a great night for us. Go home, get dressed and I'll be there in an hour."

Before she could respond, he kissed her again. Hand in hand, they stood and he walked her to the car.

Sterling had already made room for Jewel in his heart. Now it was time to truly make room for her in his life.

Chapter 23

"Jewel! How have you been? I haven't heard from you." Kevin's voice boomed through the car speakers.

"Hey, Kevin. Work, work and more work. You know how it goes. Plus my sister Chloe is getting married so that has taken up a lot of extra time." *And Sterling.* Jewel wiggled at the thought of his name. Flashes of them in his bed blazed a hot trail of delicious thoughts across her mind. "So what's up with you?"

"Ah you know—moving business along. Which brings me to why I called. Did you get my latest package?"

"I did."

"And." Kevin stretched the word over several beats.

"I still haven't made a decision. I just got a promotion at work and things have been really busy. Honestly, there's a lot for me to weigh here. It's not an easy decision."

"I really need you, Jewel. Would it help if I made the pot even sweeter?"

"Tempting, Kevin. Very tempting."

"You'll have a new offer in your inbox by Monday. Have a great weekend."

"Kevin, I—"

"Bye now." He ended the call.

Jewel pressed her lips together, took a deep breath and exhaled. This guy wasn't trying to take no for an answer.

After a few more minutes of driving she pulled up to her sister Chloe's house and noticed Jade's car. This evening they were addressing the rest of the invitations.

"Hey gals!" Jewel hugged Jade and Chloe. "What are we drinking tonight?"

"Margaritas!" Jade held hers in the air. With a wave of her hand, she invited Jewel to follow her into the dining room where they had invitations, envelopes, stamps, stickers and response cards spread across the table.

"My kind of party. But first, I need to eat. I haven't had anything since lunch and if I put a margarita on this empty stomach these invitations might be ruined!" Jewel placed her handbag on one of the chairs.

"Yuck!" Jade scrunched her nose.

"I have a fruit platter and some cheese and crackers. If you want more than that there's leftovers in the fridge. I seared a tuna steak with some risotto and veggies last night. You're welcome to have that."

"Yes!" Jewel pumped her fist. "I love it when you make risotto. I can't seem to get it right." Before Jewel could make it to the kitchen, her phone rang.

Hearing Sterling's voice put a smile in her heart that radiated on her face. She cooed, giggled and purred for the entire short conversation. When she was done, she looked up to find Chloe and Jade staring at her in awe. The three of them exchanged knowing looks before dissolving into laughter.

"What has gotten into you?" Chloe asked suspiciously.

"Maybe the question should be *who* has gotten into you?" Jade wiggled her eyebrows.

"What?" Jewel feigned innocence.

Chloe smirked. "That was not convincing."

"I know you seemed way too happy when you first bounced in here." Jade grabbed Jewel by the hand and dragged her back to the dining room. "Still is." She sat, propped her chin on her fist and waited for Jewel to start talking.

Jewel's lips spread into a toothy grin. "Okay. It's Sterling Bishop."

"Stephan and Taylor's brother, Sterling?" Jade stretched her neck in Jewel's direction."

Jewel smiled and nodded.

"The one who just revamped our computer systems at the office?" Chloe's mouth fell open. "Does dad know?"

"Of course not!" Jewel rolled her eyes upward. "I hadn't planned on telling anyone—besides you both eventually, of course."

"Sounds like something changed."

Jewel raised her brows. "Maybe."

"Oh my goodness, Jewel. You like him. You really like him! I can tell."

"There's a lot to like about him!" Jewel unleashed a belly laugh. She was done playing coy.

"Wasn't he married before?" Chloe asked.

"Yes. And he had a little girl, right." Jade looked at Jewel for confirmation. She nodded. "I'm surprised."

"Me, too. I met his daughter."

Chloe's mouth fell open and Jade gasped.

"You're kidding."

Jewel sighed and got serious. "No. I can't believe it

myself. Dom and Harper dared me to go out with him to prove I was just being superficial about my standards for dating. I took them up on the challenge figuring he was good for a few dates and maybe even a delicious romp or two and then that would be it. Well, that wasn't it. We've been inseparable ever since. I was really nervous about meeting his daughter and almost backed out, but it was like I had to prove something to myself."

"I cannot believe what I'm hearing. Keep going." Jade motioned with her hands encouraging Jewel to continue.

"She is the cutest little thing—confident, fun and toothless. Ha!" Jewel clapped as she laughed.

"How cute." Chloe held one hand to her heart.

"What about his ex-wife?"

"I met her, too."

"You did?" Jade's mouth fell open again.

Jewel shared the exchange with them and revealed that he introduced her as his girlfriend. She didn't let on in that moment, but she knew she'd made the right decision in sticking around after meeting Kylee. Jewel also shared the fact that Sterling made it clear that he wanted to be with her. Chloe covered her mouth with her hand and Jade squealed.

"I don't know."

"What do you mean you don't know?" Chloe asked looking confused. "It's obvious that you're into him. I've never seen you like this over a man. Not even the ones who met your standard."

"I know. It's almost scary. Besides being a dad and ex-husband, he's perfect. Sterling is so intelligent, sweet, thoughtful and handsome! But…"

"Are you hesitant to bring him around Mom and Dad?"

"Eh. I already know Mom is going to have a fit about

it. He's not of our pedigree even though he has a successful business. He's not from a wealthy family. The fact that he has a kid will probably make her heart stop for a while. But, Dad." Jewel paused. "Sterling used to stop by to see me in the office all the time and once Dad walked in unexpectedly. We hadn't done anything of course, but I still felt like a kid who had gotten caught in the room with a boy. Sterling stopped dropping in after that. And just so you know, we didn't go out on our first date until after the work was completed."

"I don't see what the problem is. You're the one who told me to live my life on my own terms and now I'm getting married to the most amazing man ever."

"Don't look at me," Jade said. "I got my rebellious ways from you. If you want to date the man, have at him. At least you'll get to see what kind of father he'll be if you stay together."

"If being with him makes you feel good inside and out, go for it. Everything else will fall into place. As long as he's treating you right, sooner or later, Mom and Dad will get on the bandwagon."

"You're both right." Jewel sighed. "I can't believe I'm doing this!"

"Oh! You should invite him to the wedding!" Chloe said, like it was the best idea she'd come up with all year.

"Yes!" Jade cosigned.

Little did they know, Jewel had already thought about asking Sterling.

Chapter 24

Sterling wished the summer would slow down just a little. Now that Kylee would be leaving again by the end of August, Sterling felt as if the days were passing far too quickly. He'd taken time off to spend with Kylee. Trips to the beach, amusement parks, Broadway shows and a day playing tourist in New York City made him exhausted but yielded delight beyond anything he could have imagined. Kylee belted tunes from the show all the way to Jewel's house and Sterling joined in. Every time he messed up the words or went off key, Kylee would cackle until the sound dissipated from her little body. Sterling continued butchering the songs purposely just to hear the music her giggles created.

Jewel opened the door at the same time Kylee and Sterling made it up the walk. Kylee leaped into her arms and hugged her neck. Jewel swung her around. Sterling's heart swelled a little more. Jewel would be an amazing mother. Sterling sniffed a small chuckle at the ambitious thought. Where had it come from? He wasn't ready for more kids just yet.

One good look at Jewel and warmth spread over Sterling. Bone-straight, jet-black hair framed her beautiful face. Plump red lips called out to him. Sterling fought the urge to kiss the soft, glowing skin of her bare shoulders. The light fragrance she wore delicately caressed his sense of smell. The black strapless romper gave her a sexy, yet comfortable look.

Sterling could tell she was a bit nervous by the way she fiddled with her fingers. "No need to be nervous. My family is super cool."

Jewel stood straighter. "I'm not nervous."

"You're not?"

"Of course I am. Who isn't nervous about meeting their boyfriend's parents?" She huffed.

"You'll be fine. Let's go."

During the drive, Sterling noticed how stark the differences in their neighborhoods were. Jewel, being from the North Shore, lived among lush greenery and spacious lots with grand homes set far back from the side of the road. Sterling's South Shore community was a typical suburban neighborhood with tree-lined streets, sidewalks and modest cozy homes set a short distance from one another. Kids whizzed down the road on bicycles. Couples walked with strollers, waving at their neighbors. The sounds of a summer on a Sunday afternoon filled the atmosphere. The mouthwatering aroma of a barbecue flavored the air.

The closer they got to his parents' home, the more anxious Sterling became. He knew his family would love Jewel. It was another step in confirming they were meant for each other. He wasn't worried about her father. He'd already earned his respect. Of course, dating his daughter was different, but Sterling was sure Bobby Dale would be okay with her seeing a stand-up kind of guy who didn't shy away from his responsibilities.

A nervous smiled passed Jewel's lips when Sterling pulled over to the curb. He squeezed her hand.

"We're here."

The second Sterling put the car in Park Kylee leaped out and went running through the open white gate toward the backyard.

Sterling rounded the car, opened the passenger door and helped Jewel out. Then he reached into the back seat for the cake box that Jewel had brought from her grandparents' restaurant and bakery.

Jewel flashed Sterling a pensive gaze. He took her hand once again. "Ready?"

Jewel inhaled and released the air slowly. "As ready as I'll ever be. Let's do this."

Sterling laughed. Jewel's wit was one of his many favorite things about her.

Sterling led Jewel through the gate into the yard and was bombarded with greetings by his entire family. Kylee was off somewhere in the back of the house.

"Hey, sweetie!" Patti buried Sterling in her embrace and then took the cake box he was holding.

Sterling planted a loud kiss on his mother's cheek.

"How's it going, son?" Charles embraced Sterling and patted him on the back.

"What's up, big head?" Taylor swatted him.

"Dude!" That was all Stephan said before slapping his brother five.

Everyone stood still with anxious grins anticipating Sterling's introduction. For an awkward moment they stared in awe as if she were on display at a museum. Sterling laughed. "Family!" he announced, shifting everyone's attention at once. "This is my girlfriend, Jewel. Jewel this is my mother, Patti Bishop, my dad, Charles Bishop, and my sister and brother, Taylor and Stephan, whom I think you may already know."

"Yes. It's a pleasure to meet you all. Thank you for having me."

Now Jewel was met with a barrage of greetings. Patti hugged her, Charles and Stephan offered cordial handshakes and nods and finally Taylor tilted her head and smiled.

"Nice to meet you," Taylor said. "Please excuse us, we're not creepy. We're just excited to meet someone that Sterling brought home to the family. I hope we didn't make you feel like an exotic animal behind a glass wall at the zoo. Ha!" Taylor took Jewel by the hand. "Don't be scared. We really are normal folk." Her laugh followed them all the way to the backyard.

Sterling couldn't help but laugh at his family's obvious enthusiasm. He assumed it was due to the fact that he'd only brought one woman around to meet his family since Raven—and that short-lived relationship properly forecasted by his mother and sister ended abruptly. He could tell right away that they liked Jewel.

When Sterling got to the back of the house the women went inside and the men were seated under the gazebo. Knowing that he wouldn't gain access to Jewel now that his mother and sister had swept her away, he joined his father and brother.

"You're right. I do remember her from high school. She was pretty cool."

"She's still pretty cool." Sterling winked at Stephan.

"Nice looking young lady," their dad noted.

"I'd say so."

"Shoot. She's a little more than nice looking," Stephan added. "And right now, she's alone with our sister and mother."

The three of them seemed to immediately connect in thought.

"Yeah," Charles said slowly, raising a brow. "She's probably under some kind of interrogation. You might want to check in on her." Charles snickered.

Sterling posted his hands on the arms of the chair he sat in and lifted himself up. "I think you're right."

Sterling found the three of them in the kitchen. Kylee was in the dining room playing a game on her tablet.

"Mmm." Patti's eyes were closed and her head lifted to the ceiling. She held an empty fork and with her other hand cupped under it. "Now that was good. What does your grandma call that one?"

"Lemonade pound cake."

"Let me taste, Ma!" Taylor maneuvered closer to the cake and stuck in a fresh fork. After her bite, she pretended to roll her eyes up into her head savoring the obviously scrumptious dessert. "That is amazing," she said with her mouth still full.

"It truly is. I love that one best. She makes so many."

"We have to go to their restaurant and bakery. Make sure you give me the address before you leave." Patti put her fork down and dusted crumbs from her hands. "Come on, Taylor. Let's get this food out."

"Please let me help." Jewel grabbed a bowl of salad from the counter and followed the women to the yard.

When the table was set, the family said grace. Patti told her husband about the delicious dessert awaiting them as they passed dishes and filled their plates with grilled chicken and vegetables, roasted corn on the cob and mixed green salad with summer fruit sprinkled on top.

Jewel seemed to blend in as if she'd been a fixture within Sterling's family for years. His chest swelled with pride. It pleased him to see his family embrace Jewel this way. Conversation flowed easily from one topic to the other. Patti had even chronicled how she and Charles met after he had an accident when she had just begun to work as a claims agent. Charles worked for the utility company at the time. Both enjoyed long careers with their companies and were fairly young retirees. Now they spent most of their time traveling back and forth to their second home in Georgia where they planned to permanently retire one day.

Sterling kept watch over Jewel who seemed to be thoroughly engaged. His heart melted a little when she helped Kylee break apart her chicken wing. Everything about Jewel screamed "she's the one" to him. He hadn't thought finding "the one" was even possible. That's why he chose to put dating aside and focus on being the best father he could be. Until Jewel came around, Sterling didn't realize what he'd been missing. Besides the toe-curling sex, Jewel reminded him what the good life was all about. No matter how successful his company was or how much money he made, life without a great woman wasn't as fulfilling. Being a father filled many voids, but Sterling discovered more voids had existed when Jewel's presence began to fill them.

"Jade just got a promotion." Sterling's chest expanded a little further.

"Congratulations, honey. What are you doing now?" Patti asked over a forkful of veggies.

"Vice President of Operations," Jewel answered and then flashed Sterling a sweet smile. He winked back.

"Good for you. Congrats!" Taylor said.

"That sounds like a pretty big deal," Stephan said. "Chandler Foods is a huge company."

"Your family owns Chandlers over on the pier, too, right?" Patti asked.

"Yes, ma'am."

"I think I've seen your mother before. I'm in an organization and we had an event there a few years back."

Charles nodded in agreement. "I remember that. I was with you wasn't I?"

Patti nodded. "You sure were."

"Nice place from what I recall," Charles said.

"Yes. The view was beautiful."

Charles slapped the table with his palms, arresting everyone's attention. "Time to play some cards. You know anything about pitty pat, young lady?" he asked Jewel.

"I sure do." She wiped her mouth and put her napkin down as if she were ready for a challenge. "We used to play that with my grandma and granddad all the time. They *loved* that game. Still do."

"Well let's see what you got." Charles rubbed his hands back and forth. "Steph, go get the cards."

"Already on it!" Stephan was standing by the time his father finished his sentence.

"Oh, Jewel never shies away from a good challenge," Sterling said.

Stephan returned with the cards and the games commenced.

"Be ready," Sterling warned Jewel. "Whether winning or losing we're big-time trash talkers."

"You know I can handle it." Jewel scooted closer to the table. "Bring it on."

"I really like her." Taylor raised her hand and Jewel slapped her a high five.

Charles shuffled the cards in his hands and peered around the table. "I hope y'all are ready for a nice whipping. Put some money on the table. Five dollars a game, winner takes all."

Patti put her hand on her hip from her seat. "Then get ready to lose some bank, buddy." She dug in her pocket and slapped five dollars in the center of the table.

"Look at her—feisty! Just the way I like 'em." Charles wriggled his brows.

"Yuck! Behave, parents. We have company!"

Everyone laughed.

Charles jested through the entire first game but Jewel won. She slapped her winning pair down and held her hands up in victory. Charles leaned back holding his stomach, which quaked with his belly laugh.

"Oh, that's how you're going to treat us," Stephan said laughing so hard he could hardly get the words out. "You just met us. We can't catch a break?"

"She's a lucky girl and I'm not saying that because she managed to snag me," Sterling joked.

Jewel winked and smiled. They sat enjoying the game and each other's company until sundown. Even Kylee got in on the fun, sitting on Taylor's lap plucking cards on her behalf. When the sun had finally made its spectacular exit, Sterling stood to his feet indicating that it was time to go. Sterling helped clean up outside while the ladies carried leftovers inside.

Sterling went in to place the unopened beers in the

refrigerator and found his mother in the kitchen stacking the dishwasher.

"That was a great dinner, Mom. Thanks so much."

Patti grunted as she stood holding her lower back. "See what happens when you get younger," she teased. "Ha!" Sterling chuckled and walked toward his mother. "It's always a pleasure to cook for my family." She stopped speaking and looked around him. No one else was inside. "I like her a lot. Nice girl. Not much like her mother it seems."

"You know her mother? How?" Sterling jerked his head back.

"Met her at the event I mentioned earlier. Some of the ladies in the organization know her pretty well. I assume you have yet to meet her," Patti guessed.

"I haven't been introduced yet."

She looked around him one last time. "Be careful, son. She's a bit of a snoot!" Patti let out a sharp laugh. "You'd think she was born wearing diapers made out of dollar bills."

"Bye mom." Sterling kissed his mother's cheek. She was still laughing.

"Sterling. Can Kylee come home with me?" Taylor asked the second he stepped back outside.

"Oh. Yes! Please, Daddy. Can I go home with Auntie Taylor?"

"Sure."

"Yay!" Kylee jumped up and down.

"She has a room full of clothes at my place so she won't need anything."

Taylor's idea was perfect, Sterling thought. He'd been eyeing Jewel in that romper all day imagining ways to get her out of it. He also hadn't seen much of her during the past week so he couldn't wait to get her alone. He was happy about how the day went. Jewel impressed his family just like he knew she would with her wit and charm. He wanted to show her how much he appreciated the woman she was and that's exactly what he planned to do tonight.

After helping the family clean up, they said their good-byes. Sterling laced his fingers with Jewel's and rode home holding her hand. Once they arrived at her house, he walked her in, closing the door behind him with his foot.

"You looked beautiful today. I couldn't wait to get you alone," Sterling spoke close to her lips, kissing them between his words.

"Oh yeah. Well, what did you have planned?"

"A late night snack." Sterling picked Jewel up and carried her up to the bedroom.

Gently he laid her on the bed, kissed her face repeatedly and covered her mouth with his. She undressed him as much as she could while their lips remained connected. They parted, continued to peel each other's clothes off, flinging garments across the room. Sterling tasted every part of her smoldering skin before burring his face between her thighs. As the temperature in the room rose, so did his tempo. Hunger compelled them to move with more urgency each moment. Sterling licked her into a powerful, explosive place. Jewel thrashed around the bed, grasping at handfuls of sheets and panting his name.

Hearing Jewel call him over and over made his core tighten. His erection was like stone. Sheathing himself, he skillfully filled her to the core—her moist walls still clenched from her climax. The suctioning made Sterling's eyes roll back. Intense pleasure threatened to prematurely

take him over the edge. Sterling had to gather his strength
to steady his stride. Pleasing her was the most important thing. His satisfaction was directly linked to her joy.

Sterling found his rhythm. Their bodies collided in a
perfect syncopation. Feeling himself in the brink of control, he pulled out, sat up and lowered her onto him. In
that small amount of time, he regained his composure.
Jewel's body started to shake. The shudder started at her
center and mushroomed to every part of her. Sterling
caught the extreme wave of pleasure like it was contagious. A powerful surge of heat coursed through him.
Control completely evaded his grasp. Still shuddering,
Jewel wrapped her arms round him, squeezing as she
chanted his name breathlessly. They pounded against
each other until Sterling's entire body grew rigid and his
climax thundered through him. His groans were guttural.
His core clenched in hard waves. In each other's arms,
they reached their highest peak and collapsed against
each other. Their hearts beat in rapid succession. Lying
back on the bed, they stayed folded into each other until
drifting off into a peaceful slumber.

Chapter 25

Jewel was sure about Sterling but not so sure about him meeting her family. The idea of her mother asking Sterling questions about his pedigree riled her. She finally accepted the fact that matching upbringings didn't matter all that much. Mostly, she wondered what her father would say. She didn't want Bobby Dale thinking they had been anything but professional while Sterling's company was doing work at Chandler Food Corp.

Jewel had put this off long enough. So much so that Sterling began to question her about it. "My family is a bit complicated," is what she said. The preparation and timing had to be right. With Chloe's wedding coming in a few short weeks, she couldn't afford to wait much longer. Sterling's flight and their hotel room were already booked.

To Sterling's obvious surprise, she insisted he bring Kylee with him to dinner. She thought it best to get everything out at once. When she made the suggestion, he asked her several times if she was sure. She'd fallen for Kylee and figured if she accepted her then her family would

It Must Be Love

have to as well. After meeting Kylee they would also be smitten by her mess of curls, curious conversation and precocious charm.

Jewel stopped pacing the floor in her kitchen and laughed. As outspoken as she was, she couldn't believe how this was affecting her. What happened to the rebel?

The bell rang. She inhaled and let the air out in a rush. "Coming."

Sterling was at the door with Kylee. As usual, she leaped into Jewel's arms, but wiggled out quickly and bounced on her little toes.

Sterling gave Jewel a peck on the cheek, pointed to his jittery daughter and mouthed, "Bathroom." He ushered Kylee in the direction of the powder room.

Something swelled in Jewel's chest every time Kylee jumped into her arms. It reminded her of the Grinch's growing heart. The love that little girl lavished on Jewel from the moment she met her opened Jewel's mind and her perspective. The nightmares she'd heard about dating and marrying men with families didn't seem to hold true with Sterling.

Jewel had to admit that before Kylee even entered the picture, Sterling had her smitten. Yes, he was ultra-easy on the eyes, but it was the man inside the gorgeous casing that reeled Jewel in—his mind, his heart, his uncanny ability to please her beyond anything she'd ever experienced. Enjoying his company, having a blast in his presence and feeling like the most important priority in the world were all things that Jewel hadn't expected. No man had ever appealed to all of her sensibilities like Sterling had. His schooling and so many other things no longer mattered. What a tricky dare! The only one who seemed to have been fooled in the end was her. Yet she ended up with the prize.

"Ready," Sterling said, coming from the bathroom.

"I hope you're ready for El."

"I can handle it."

Jewel looked at him as if she wasn't so sure. "Let's do this."

Trepidation thumped in Jewel's chest during the entire ride. When they arrived at her parents' estate, she was happy to see that her siblings had already arrived. They'd all spoken earlier that day and agreed to buffer the situation in any way possible. El was much harder on her girls than her son and had fallen in love with Serenity, Chris's girlfriend, from the moment she met her. But for Chloe, Jade and Jewel any man less than what El deemed as perfect was a problem.

She came around with Donovan, but he had the right background and wealthy upbringing. Each of them managed to keep most of their dates clear of El. Jade had yet to bring someone home at all. Now it was Jewel's turn. Jewel sucked her teeth, shunning her mother's potential behavior. She hadn't realized how audible it was until Sterling asked if she was okay.

"I'm fine," she told him.

Jewel took her time getting out of the car. The rebel in her awakened. *El, this is what I want so you're going to have to deal with it.* Jewel only hoped that firmness accompanied her inside the house.

Chloe opened the door for them.

"Hi, Sterling. It's so nice to see you." Chloe embraced him. "And who is this little rock star?" Chloe spoke of Kylee but looked at Jewel.

"That's Kylee." Jewel looked directly back at Chloe. She knew Kylee's presence would startle everyone.

"Kylee, this is my big sister, Ms. Chloe."

"Hi Ms. Chloe. You're pretty just like Ms. Jewel."

"Aw!" Chloe's hand went to her heart. "Thank you, sweetie."

Jewel's next stare told Chloe "I know what I'm doing." Chloe pursed her lips and raised her brows.

Jade and Christian greeted them as they made their way to the family room. "Hey, Sterling. What's up, man?" Chris offered a firm handshake.

"Not much. How's it going?" Sterling ended the shake and patted Chris's arm.

"Nice to see you." Jade offered her hand. "And who's this little cutie?" Like Chloe, Jade turned to Jewel for an unspoken answer.

Jewel gave her the same firm expression, which defied the sweetness in her voice when she said, "This cutie's name is Kylee. She's Sterling's precious daughter. Kylee, this is my other sister. Her name is Jade."

"Well aren't you just adorable." Jade bent forward addressing Kylee face-to-face.

"Thank you, Ms. Jade. You're pretty, too, just like your sisters."

"Aw!" Jade pouted, responding just like Chloe had. "I like her already. Would you like some juice, sweetie?" Kylee nodded. "Come with me. Your dress is so pretty." Jade's voice trailed off as she walked away with Kylee.

Chloe turned to Jewel with a serious expression. "Mom's in the dining room picking over the table setting."

"It's go time!" Jewel said, taking Sterling's hand and leading him to where her mother was. "Mom. Dad. We're here."

"I'm in here, honey."

Jewel followed El's voice. "Dad. Where are you?"

"Coming, sweetie."

They all converged in the dining room. El hugged Jewel and lifted her chin in Sterling's direction.

"This is my friend Sterling Bishop," Jewel said, hoping Sterling wouldn't be upset with her referring to him as her friend.

El offered him a cool "Hello."

"Hey, Sterling! How have you been, young man?"

"Doing well, Mr. Chandler. It's a pleasure to be in your home. How are things with you, sir?"

"Well you know—a little bit of this and a little bit of that. Come on in the other room with me."

Sterling followed Bobby Dale. His welcome made Jewel smile. When she turned back to El, her smile fell.

"Tell me about this young man. Where is he from? Who is his family?"

Before Jewel could begin to respond Kylee burst into a fit of giggles. The sound cut through the tension in the room. Jewel couldn't help her smile. Kylee's laughter could warm an ice queen's heart. Jade's laughter lifted and joined in with Kylee's. El and Jewel headed to the kitchen to see what was happening.

In the kitchen, Jade and Kylee were bent over. Jade held her side. Kylee's eyes were almost shut from laughing so hard. Jade gathered herself and pointed at Kylee. "This kid does the best impressions."

El moved Jewel out of the way and slowly walked toward Kylee, looking at her as if she were trying to figure out how she materialized. She looked back at Jewel. "Who is this child?"

Jewel stood erect, lifted her chin, walked over to

Kylee and gently placed a hand on her upper back. Kylee stopped laughing abruptly. Her large eyes moved back and forth between El and Jewel and then landed on Jewel with a look of worry. Jade placed her hand over Kylee's.

"This little sweetheart is Sterling's daughter. Kylee, this is my mommy Mrs. Elnora Chandler."

"Oh." El didn't crack a smile nor did her face soften. "Hello." The greeting was as devoid of warmth as the one El doled out to the girl's father.

After a few awkward seconds, Kylee spoke. "Hi Mrs. El…nora."

Chloe cleared her throat. "Why don't we go into the great room?"

"No." Everyone's head snapped in El's direction. "Dinner is ready. We can go into the dining room." She spun around and called for Leah, their housekeeper. "We're ready now."

"Hi ladies." Leah seemed to come from nowhere. She waved at Jewel and Kylee. "Yes, ma'am." She nodded at El and disappeared as quickly as she appeared.

The family gathered around the massive dining table. After a brief grace, silence took over as plates were filled. There was an air of apprehension. No one seemed to want to start a conversation. The only sounds in the room were forks clanging against plates and glasses connecting with coasters. Even the sound of cutting meat could be heard because it was so quiet.

"That was a great job you did for us at the office, Sterling."

"Thank you, Mr. Chandler. It was a pleasure working with your staff."

"Alex was great! He was thorough and explained everything to us." Jewel added.

"I'll call you when it's time to upgrade our systems over at our restaurant," Bobby Dale offered.

"Sounds good. We'll be sure to take care of you, sir."

"I'm sure you will."

"So. Sterling… How's business been going? Seems your company continues to grow pretty fast," Chris asked.

"It's great, actually. We just made the top ten list of emerging companies on Long Island. After the article, the phones started ringing off the hook. I can't complain. It's a great problem to have." Sterling cut a piece of filet mignon and placed it in his mouth. "This is delicious, Mrs. Chandler."

"Thank you."

Quiet settled around El's short response. Until then El eyed Sterling and Kylee curiously, not adding much to the conversation going around the table.

"Sterling." She called his name and everyone at the table looked up as if she called them.

"Yes, ma'am."

"Where is your family from?"

"Freeport."

"Oh!" El looked taken aback and glanced at Jewel. "I don't think I know any Bishops. And how old is this precious little girl?"

"I'm six!" Kylee said proudly.

"Yes. She's six."

"Oh. And do I understand correctly that you attended school with my children?"

"Yes."

El tilted her head. Jewel held her breath and was pretty sure her siblings were doing the same. "What's the professions of your parents?"

"They're retired now and pretty hard to keep up with. My mother was a claims agent for an insurance company and my father worked for the utility company."

"And they sent you to Oxford?" El jerked her head back. She seemed genuinely confused.

Jewel didn't stop the line of questioning for two reasons. One it would prove futile and two, she was certain that Sterling could handle himself. He didn't seem bothered one bit.

"Yes. Both my siblings and me."

"Oh." El looked more confused.

Jewel could see the wheels churning in El's mind, wondering how average working parents on the South Shore managed to send three kids to one of the most expensive and prestigious prep schools on Long Island. Remaining quiet, Jewel waited for what she knew was coming.

"Did you *all* receive a scholarship?"

"In fact we did. The school wanted me because of my athleticism and grades and offered to take the three of us. We were all members of the honor society and pretty keen at sports and music."

"Well…that's very nice." El didn't seem impressed at all. "Tell me more about your company."

Sterling obliged, relaying the story of how he and his brother came up with the idea and started the business.

"Hmm." El put her fork down and looked directly at him. "And your daughter's mother…where is she?"

"Chicago, pursuing her PhD."

"Interesting. So Kylee lives with you?"

"I have her during school breaks and summers."

"I see."

Sterling smiled and put down his fork. "With all due

respect Mrs. Chandler." Jewel's stomach tightened at his words. "I completely understand your concern. I'm a self-made man who comes from a great, modest and loving family. I married my girlfriend because we thought it was the right thing to do. We realized shortly after that it wasn't the best move and now our goal is to be the best parents we can be for this amazing little girl." Sterling looked at Kylee and his adoration for her was evident. She smiled back. "I'm rather careful in dealing with women since my daughter can be quite impressionable. There's something very special about Jewel and we'd love to see where our relationship will take us. I only hope we're able to do that with your blessing. I'm pleased to answer any of your questions. Rest assured, I'm well able to care for your daughter in every way possible."

Jewel wanted to jump into his lap and kiss his entire face. That wouldn't have gone over well with her mother or her dad. Instead she squirmed proudly in her seat, hoping it went unnoticed. She glanced up in time to catch both Jade and Chloe's lips quiver slightly, holding back smiles.

El eyed him for several moments without responding. "And I'll be watching."

Sterling smiled. "If I had a daughter as incredible as Jewel, I'd watch closely, too."

Bobby Dale sat back. "Young man. You remind me a lot of myself."

Jewel breathed a sigh of relief. It meant the world to her that Bobby Dale respected Sterling. El would eventually come around—she hoped.

After dinner, they dropped Kylee by Sterling's mother's house and headed back to his place. Jewel planned to show Sterling how proud she was of the way he handled himself with her parents. Instead they fell asleep, tangled in each other's arms after binge-watching a season of one of Jewel's favorite shows.

Chapter 26

Sterling kissed Jewel's face until she awakened. Stiff with desire, he pressed his erection against her side and smiled as she squeezed her eyes shut against the glow of the morning sun. Sterling pecked her lids.

"You sure can sleep."

Jewel covered her mouth. "You sure know how to keep a girl up at night."

Sterling winked. His erection flinched as he remembered the night before. He'd made love to Jewel until both were slumped across the bed—no energy left for anything but slumber. He woke in the morning, still naked with the lingering scent of sex clinging to their bodies.

Sterling ran his finger across her nose and mouth. Jewel puckered, kissing the tip of it as it passed her lips.

"Tell me how you did it," Sterling said.

"How I did what?" Jewel wrinkled her nose.

"Get here. Now. With me. Making me not want to be anywhere else in this world."

Jewel smirked and shimmied, shuffling the bed sheets. "I'm irresistible."

Sterling's head fell back as he laughed. "True, but seriously, I've asked myself so many times. How did we get here?"

"I know what you mean." Jewel looked into his eyes.

Sterling leaned forward and kissed her. His eyes closed instinctively as he savored the feel of her soft lips. Something happened—a foreign but wonderful feeling mushroomed in his chest. Sterling had never felt that way about a woman in his life. Without scaring her off, he needed to tell her how serious this was for him. He couldn't see himself without her.

"After my divorce, I avoided dating for a long time. I thought it would distract me from being a good dad. Being a divorced man and an active father wasn't easy. I'd seen many other men have issues managing new relationships with exes and children. I had tried and it didn't go well. Then I avoided getting too involved with woman and kind of 'moved on' when things looked like they could get serious. But then you came along. With you I wanted to take the risk."

Jewel's stare was intense. Sterling tried to choose his words carefully.

"I wanted you. I wanted you to accept Kylee and for Kylee to accept you and with that, I'd have the approval to move forward." Sterling paused to let his words sink in. He watched Jewel blink and swallow and continue to stare back at him wordlessly. "Do you think you can handle Kylee and me on a long-term basis?"

Jewel's neck shifted like a lever. She swallowed again and cleared her throat.

"I didn't want to."

Her candor struck him.

"When I heard that you had a daughter, I immediately ruled you out, but that obviously became hard to stick with. Then I met her." Jewel smiled "And she's just as amazing as you. I won't lie. I still struggle with it at times. I never wanted to deal with the problems that come with exes when children are involved. I can't see living with that type of drama." Jewel huffed. "But I'm here."

Sterling appreciated her honesty. "I'm glad you're still here and I plan to take advantage of that right now." Laughing, he slid his arm under her body and pulled Jewel to him. He didn't underestimate what it took for Jewel to stick around.

Again, Sterling pressed himself against her, waking his erection. He held his body over hers and planted several pecks on her lips. She puckered but kept her mouth tight.

"Who cares about your morning breath?"

Jewel giggled under her palm. "Me!"

Sterling moved her hand away and kissed her passionately until she relented. An immediate wave of heat washed over him. Ravenous kisses explored her mouth, down her torso, between her legs and back up to her lips. Her scorching skin seemed to sizzle under his touch. Jewel wrapped her arms and legs around his back. Her own back arched hard. He craved her. His taste for her was insatiable. Sterling guided himself into her cavern. A gasp. A hiss. Jewel moaned deep in her throat. She grabbed him from behind. Pulled him to her. Their tempo was insistent. Grunts and groans collided. A sensual, guttural cacophony ensued. A clamoring crescendo was reached. They collapsed—sated, panting until they could just breathe. Jewel snuggled against him. Sterling held her closer.

Sterling knew they had to get out of the bed, but being

wrapped in her arms felt too good. He savored the moment for a little while longer, glad that she was there. He knew accepting him and Kylee and even Raven as a package wasn't easy. Yet she'd met his parents and he'd met hers and at that very moment, Jewel was in his arms. Sterling made careful decisions and Jewel was one of them.

"What time is it?" Jewel asked after a while.

"We should probably be showered by now. The bouncy house guys should be here any minute."

Jewel propelled forward, squinting toward the clock on his nightstand. "Sterling! We'd better get up. There's so much to do before Kylee gets here."

"Come here." Sterling pulled her back down to him and held her one more time. "Now let's go," he said, as if that was what he needed to get going.

Jewel shook her head, got up and started for the adjoining bath. "Race you to the shower."

"Cheater."

"Ha!" Jewel's laugh trailed behind her.

They dressed and sprang into action, running all the necessary errands for Kylee's birthday party. When they returned. The bouncy house was set up in the yard and the receipt was in the mailbox.

By the time Taylor and his mother, Patti, arrived with Kylee, the rest of their family was in the yard, burgers and hot dogs were on the grill and music flowed through the outdoor space. A few kids from the neighborhood whom Kylee played with before going to Chicago with Raven joined the festivities. Kids with painted faces like cute animals laughed when Jewel joined their dance contest. Kylee gushed and took to the center of the circle with Jewel and they danced together. Contagious giggles wafted in the air.

The entire scene brought warmth to Sterling's heart and a broad smile to his face until he looked over and saw that Raven was the only one on the patio who wasn't smiling.

Sterling flipped the last burger and headed inside to bring out the rest of the food his mother had made so everyone could eat.

"Hey."

"What's up?" Sterling said over his shoulder as Raven followed him inside. She'd arrived back in New York that day to attend Kylee's party just like she had for the past two years.

"Nice job on the party this year. It's so much bigger."

"Yeah. I had a little more help with the planning." Sterling put the pan with the burgers on the countertop and covered them with aluminum foil.

"Your girlfriend seems nice."

"Yes. She is." Sterling kept milling about, gathering the cold items from the refrigerator. He thought about calling Taylor inside to help but sensed that Raven had more to say than how nice Jewel seemed.

"I wanted to talk to you."

"I figured as much. What about?"

"Her."

Sterling stopped moving and tilted his head. "What about *her*?" He and Raven had never truly been in love. This couldn't be jealousy. Sterling wondered what she was up to.

"I'm just concerned."

"About what?" Now Sterling faced her.

"How long have you known her? How long have you two been dating? You never mentioned her before that day at your house."

"Raven!" Sterling placed the oven mitts in the counter. "Where is this coming from? We've never done this." He waved his hand around.

"What do you mean by this?"

"We've never questioned each other about our lives. You've been dating since you got to Chicago. I've never interrogated you about your boyfriends."

"Because I never introduced them to Kylee."

"Oh!" Sterling paced a circle in the kitchen floor. "Do you think I'd just bring any kind of woman around our daughter?"

"I'm not saying that."

"Then what…" Sterling paused and lowered his voice. "What are you saying?"

"I told you, I'm just concerned. I've never heard of you dating this woman before and the first time I run into her, you tell me she's your girlfriend. You have her around our daughter…" Raven stammered. "Obviously all of the time since Kylee seems to know her so well," she spat sarcastically, her frustration now on display. "Kylee is my daughter. If you're going to have this woman around her you should have said something to me. She just pops out of nowhere and I'm supposed to be okay with that."

"Ra—!" The second part of her name failed to pass his lips when he looked past Raven and saw Jewel standing in the door with hot dog buns in her hand.

Raven rolled her eyes upward and lowered her head. Jewel stared past Raven and directly into Sterling's eyes. His mouth opened but nothing came out. The tension in the air was thick and noxious like smoke. Closing the space between them, Jewel took calculated steps toward Sterling. She placed the rolls in his hands.

"The girls asked for hot dogs."

With that she turned and walked outside. Sterling knew that her exit was bigger than just her physically passing through the door.

Chapter 27

"Jewel!"

"Huh? What?"

"I called you like six times," Jade groaned.

"What's going on, Jewel? You're not with us today," Harper said.

"Oh. It's nothing." Jewel shrugged. "I'm fine."

"You don't look fine." Dominique sat on the settee next to Jewel. "You look like a sick puppy sitting here staring out this window."

"You guys are ganging up on me?" she teased, but didn't feel as light as she portrayed.

"Chloe is looking for you," Jade said.

"And she sent out a search party."

"Pretty much." Jade squatted in front of her. "What's wrong, Jewel? You haven't been yourself all week."

"I'm just tired. This bridal shower was a lot of work." She tried putting her mood off on the shower but the twisted lips and sideways glances she received from her sister and friends showed her they weren't buying it. Jewel breathed deeply and released it with a groan.

"Really, I'm fine. Let's get back outside before Chloe comes looking for all of us." She looked at her watch. "It's time to open the gifts. We'll need to wrap this up before our time runs out. Help me grab the rest of these gift bags so we can hand them out as people leave." Jewel pointed at the favors on the parlor floor at the old Victorian Hillcrest Mansion, but hung back as the girls took handfuls out with them.

They'd rented the venue out for Chloe's bridal shower because it offered the perfect setting for a vintage tea party. Each attendee donned a hat and fascinators in honor of the theme. Several tables were set up outside in the center of the garden. Vases filled with fresh-cut flowers served as centerpieces with fine china expertly set around the table. Despite the beauty surrounding them and the cheerful vibe permeating the atmosphere, Jewel couldn't shake her mood.

Sterling called later the night of Kylee's party, suggesting they talk. That's when she'd given in to her fear and told him she didn't think a relationship between them would work. Sterling tried to convince her otherwise and said he'd talked with Raven as well but Jewel was insistent. She spent much of the week kicking herself for falling for Sterling in spite of his situation.

It turned out to be exactly what she attempted to avoid in the first place.

If she allowed herself to be completely honest, she'd admit to being heartbroken. Sterling had etched himself into so many aspects of her life. Now that he was no longer around, she felt the hollowness of all the empty spaces his absence created. Several times, she'd absentmindedly picked up the phone to run an idea by him. Jewel would call him and then end the call a moment later when she remembered that what they had was no more. The night before she reached for him in her sleep and woke with a start when her arm landed on the empty side of the bed.

Jewel surprised herself with how much she'd come to care for him in such a short period of time. It was definitely going to take time to eject Sterling from her system.

"Jewel," Chloe called softly. "Are you okay?"

"Sure." She tried to sound convincing. "I was just making sure we got everything out of this room before it was time to leave." Jewel stopped milling about long enough to take Chloe in. Her coral tea-length dress made her look innocent. "Happiness looks good on you, sis. You look beautiful."

"Thank you. It was looking good on you, too."

"Was?" Jewel was heading toward the door but halted and looked back at Chloe.

"Yes." Chloe placed her hand on Jewel's shoulder. "Have you spoken with Sterling?"

Jewel sighed. "No."

Chloe pursed her lips. "It's clear that you guys have something special. Don't give up on it too easily."

Jewel forced a smile but couldn't promise her sister that she wasn't going to walk away.

"Come on." Chloe took her by the hand. "We can talk about that later. Right now, we're supposed to be having fun." Chloe led Jewel back to the garden where the festivities were taking place.

For the remainder of the shower, Jewel tried her best to settle into the fun, but couldn't keep her mind from straying. To stay focused, she busied herself cleaning up the wrappers after the gifts were opened, tidying up and tending to Chloe.

On her way home, she found herself absentmindedly making a turn toward Sterling's direction. With a grunt, she made a U-turn and headed home. So much of her routine was automated around him. Once she made it inside, she almost called to let him know she'd made it safely. She even missed Kylee—her cute giggle, their silly dance routines and most of all her warm, tight hugs. Yet she refused to go into a situation with the challenges of a man with an ex-wife and child. Relationships were hard enough to maintain without interference—especially if they were potentially problematic. She recalled the small part of Raven and Sterling's conversation. It was clear that Raven wasn't happy about her being in Sterling and Kylee's life. As the mother of his child, Raven would undoubtedly have a strong influence on their relationship.

After a fitful night of minimal sleep, Jewel woke tired. When the jolt of two cups of strong coffee finally kicked in, she decided that's just what she needed in life as well—a refreshing restart. When she got to work, she was going to call Kevin and set up a meeting about the offer. She would have to work on letting Sterling go, as well. Her feelings were too tender to consider a friendship. Since it couldn't be all, it would have to be nothing until she could handle more interaction with him.

By the time Jewel reached the office, she'd worked herself into a new perspective. She called Kevin and to his disappointment declined his job offer and his immediate attempt to counter. Kevin had let her know that he understood and respected her decision.

Jewel then composed an email to Sterling expressing her feelings and apologies for not being able to be with him. Whether or not to send it was a decision she would make later. Right now, the purpose was to help her work through her emotions. She didn't feel any happier, but did feel less heavy. Maybe she'd send it someday.

The last thing she did before diving into work was call Chloe to apologize for putting a damper on her special day.

"No apologies necessary, sis," Chloe insisted. "Not so long ago, I was where you are—missing Donovan and trying to figure out the best way to move on without him. I couldn't lie to myself. I wanted to be with Donovan despite what other people thought, including Mom. I made my decision for me and I just hope you do the same."

"Thanks, Chloe."

Chloe's comment completely unraveled Jewel's well-laid reasoning for walking away clean. She knew what her heart wanted, but wasn't willing to tolerate what it would take to make things work. She ended her day the same way she started it—torn.

Chapter 28

Spending the day with Kylee at the water park gave Sterling so much joy despite still feeling dejected about the way things were going with Jewel. As they exited the park, Sterling looked in on Kylee sitting in the back seat playing games on a tablet. Usually he kept the radio on but right now he wasn't in the mood for music. Running around that water park with Kylee wore him out, but it wasn't fatigue that caused his quieted disposition. He couldn't escape his thoughts of Jewel.

"Daddy, are you okay?" Kylee was perceptive for such a young girl. She'd always been attuned to Sterling's temperament.

"Yes, sweetie. I'm fine."

"So why do you seem sad? We were just having so much fun."

"No reason."

"Will I get to see Ms. Jewel again before I leave?"

"I don't know, honey."

"Is she mad at you? Is that why she hasn't come around? Do you miss her? I know I do."

Sterling shook his head and smiled. "Yeah. I miss her." He decided to be honest.

Kylee launched a bunch more questions barely giving him time to respond. Sterling steered the conversation toward getting ready for school. By the time they reached the interstate, Kylee was slumped in her car seat, fast asleep. A smile generated from his heart when he glanced back at her sleeping form.

It saddened him that she would be leaving him in another week to head back to Chicago. He'd have to endure a few more years of seeing his daughter only on holidays, school breaks and summers until Raven graduated again. Sterling wasn't happy about it at all, but understood Raven's position and her refusal to allow Kylee to stay in New York. Truthfully, Sterling didn't really expect Raven to leave Kylee behind. Trusting him wasn't the issue. It was hard to separate a good mother from her daughter and Raven's flexible schedule would allow her to spend more time with Kylee than Sterling could. Much of his time was consumed by his business and he'd have to rely heavily on his family to pitch in and help out with Kylee if she stayed with him. After much debate, Raven and Sterling finally agreed on Kylee returning to Chicago with Raven.

The open road made way for contemplation. The silence inside the car became overwhelming. Sterling still wasn't in the mood for music, but his thoughts kept circling back to Jewel. Several times in the past few days he fought the urge to show up at her door. There was so much more to say, but until he could guarantee that she wouldn't have to deal with problems from Raven, he'd keep his distance for now. Somehow, he was going to find a way to fix this. Letting Jewel walk out of his life wasn't an option.

Sterling thought back to the night of the reunion and how stunning Jewel looked. Only a few months had passed since then, but with Jewel at his side, those had been the most thrilling months of his life since the birth of his daughter. Outside of Kylee and his family, Sterling managed to carve out a lonely existence before Jewel came along adding flavor with her presence. Her mind intrigued him. Her body stimulated him. Their conversations went on for hours. She was witty, charming, intelligent, beautiful, ambitious—the list went on. He didn't want to give that up. Not yet. Anything worth having was worth working for and if Sterling had to put in some work to get Jewel back in his life, then he was willing.

Sterling's thoughts moved to Raven. He still found her behavior at Kylee's party upsetting. He felt like she'd accused him of being an irresponsible father. And the party wasn't the ideal place to have that discussion anyway. Though they came to terms on their daughter's living arrangements, they'd yet to see eye to eye on Raven's questions about his relationship with Jewel.

These thoughts accompanied him back to his neighborhood. Glancing in the rearview mirror, he smiled at Kylee shifting in her sleep. His mother often said that children saw through to the truth of a person. Somehow they were more keenly attuned to their intuition than adults. Even as a baby, there were certain people that Kylee instinctively didn't like. She'd cry whenever they were around and would kick and scream if they tried to pick her up. As much as that inquisitive little girl loved to chat, she still became quiet around people she didn't take to. Yet Kylee and Jewel connected immediately. Even she knew that Jewel was special.

Sterling made a left instead of a right at the next corner and drove to his parents' home. The first step toward getting Jewel back was to have a candid conversation with Raven. He wasn't willing to waste another moment. Sterling dialed Raven's number.

"Hi. We need to talk. Can I stop by?"

Raven didn't respond immediately. "Sure." Her sigh was evident through the phone. They had returned to a place where communicating was an awkward dance.

"I'm on my way now."

Within fifteen minutes, Sterling had dropped off Kylee and was in front of Raven's three-story complex where she kept her New York apartment. He exited the car with conviction. Sterling had business to take care of.

Raven opened the door and walked to her kitchen without a greeting. Sterling followed her inside.

Pulling the refrigerator open she asked if Sterling wanted anything. She'd yet to look at him.

"I'm fine." He needed to get straight to the reason for his visit.

Raven grabbed a bottle of water and joined him at the dining table.

"What did you want to talk about?"

"Jewel."

Raven took a deep breath and exhaled a rush of air. "What about her?"

"I don't know why—"

Raven held her hand up, stopping him. "Wait. Let me try to explain this again. I don't care who you date and I'm not judging your fathering skills. If you're serious about this woman and she's going to be around our child

I just think that I deserved some kind of notice. I'm not saying you need my approval, but a heads-up would have been fair. That's all. I may have come off the wrong way, but that was the point I was trying to make."

Sterling nodded. "That's fair."

"You know I'd never try to dictate how you should live your life or whom you spend your time with. You've always been an amazing dad. If Jewel is who you want to be with, so be it. When I saw how well she and Kylee got along, I became concerned—for Kylee, not me."

"I love my daughter and I care about Jewel a lot. I really want things to work out with us, and now realize that all of us will have to play a part in making that happen. I'm glad we spoke."

Both of them remained quiet for several moments. "She seems nice," Raven said after a while.

"She's great!" Sterling couldn't help his smile.

"Are you compatible?"

"In so many ways."

"Unlike us." She chuckled. "That's good."

Sterling stood. "I'm glad I came by."

"Me, too." Raven smiled. This seemed like a step toward their restoring their friendship.

"I need to go. I'll see you next week when I drop Kylee off."

"Cool." Raven followed him to the door.

Instead of going straight back to get Kylee, Sterling called his sister, Taylor, to see if she was home and then swung by there.

"You caught me at a good time. Want a beer?" She pulled two out of the refrigerator before he answered.

Sterling took it.

"How's Jewel?"

"That's what I wanted to talk to you about."

"Mmm." Taylor took a swig of beer and sat on the stool in front of her breakfast nook. She pointed to the stool next to her but Sterling preferred to stand. "She didn't look very happy leaving Kylee's party last week."

He leaned against the counter. "She wasn't. She walked in on a conversation between me and Raven that wasn't going so well."

"Oh. That's not good." Taylor scrunched her face.

"It wasn't. We spoke the day after and she basically said she was sorry but couldn't do this—meaning us. I've reached out a few times after that, but we've yet to speak."

"Uh-uh." Taylor shook her head slowly.

"Even Kylee misses her."

"I know she's important to you. How do you plan on fixing this?"

"With your help."

"I can tell you what she's thinking."

"What!"

"She doesn't want to engage in any *baby-mama-drama*."

Sterling tilted his head and eyed Taylor narrowly. He hated that expression.

"Really. And she shouldn't have to. That's your past not hers. As long as she accepts Kylee as part of the package she shouldn't have to worry about problems with Raven. That's for you to manage. What was Raven's issue, anyway?"

"She said I should have mentioned the fact that Jewel and I were getting serious since she's Kylee's mother."

"She's right, too."

"I didn't get where she was coming from at first, but

I spoke to her today and she explained what she meant. I get it now. I just have to figure out how to get Jewel to speak with me in order to clear this up."

"And you're going to have to be convincing and impressive."

"That's where you and your big ideas come in."

Taylor tapped her jaw. "Let me see what I can come up with." She stood. "Call me in the morning. Right now, I need to get ready for my date."

"With who?" Sterling stood. His eyebrows knitted.

"Calm down, cowboy! I'm a big girl remember?" She rolled her eyes. "Brothers. Geesh!"

Sterling laughed, releasing some of the tension that had built up in recent days. "You'll always be my little sister."

Taylor turned him around and nudged him in the direction of the door. "Bye, big brother."

Chapter 29

"You seem sad, Daddy." Kylee climbed on Sterling's lap and nestled her head on his chest.

Sterling kissed the top of her head. "What makes you say that?" He really didn't need to ask. He hadn't meant for his pensive state to show enough for Kylee to notice. Sterling hadn't come up with a way to reach Jewel yet.

"You're quiet."

Sterling ruffled the mess of curls jutting from her ponytail. "Are you trying to say I'm usually loud?"

"No!" Kylee snickered. "Well…"

"What!" Sterling tickled her. Kylee's fit of giggles reached all the way to his core, triggering a spark in his spirit. Kylee laughed until no sound escaped her. Sterling kissed her forehead.

After a while Kylee settled down and studied her dad. "Why hasn't Ms. Jewel been around?"

"Time for bed, sweetie. Tomorrow is a big day. We've got a lot to do before your meeting up with Mommy at the airport. Why don't you ahead and take your shower."

"Okay, Daddy." Kylee rolled her eyes. Sterling laughed, awed at how insightful his daughter had become.

Kylee slid from Sterling's lap. "Go on now." Instead of following Kylee, Sterling went to the refrigerator and took out a beer. Leaning against the counter, he popped the can open and chugged. He poured the rest of the beer down the sink, pulled a bottle of Merlot from the wine cooler and poured a glass. Placing the wine on the table, he sat as he sipped slowly, relishing the full-bodied essence of the wine.

Sterling needed to see Jewel and talk face-to-face. He would walk away when he was sure that there was no chance for them. He didn't believe it was over just yet. Letting her go without one last try would leave him with regrets—something Sterling vowed to avoid to the best of his ability.

What did he want from Jewel? Sterling asked himself. Why couldn't he just walk away? He knew the answer. Jewel wasn't just beautiful, she was everything that he imagined the perfect woman could be, but didn't quite believe truly existed. Her mind intrigued him. Her scent implored him. Her sense of adventure excited him, but most of all, she adored Kylee. He wouldn't even think about the way his body responded to being in her company. Jewel's absence affected him as much as her presence. He no longer felt complete without her around. Sterling cared for Jewel more than he could ever recall caring for any woman. The next thought propelled him to his feet. Sterling loved Jewel. In the short time they'd been together, she'd captured his heart—a feat he'd considered impossible.

Sterling took his glass to the den with him to retrieve his cell phone. It wasn't on the table where he thought he'd left it. Sterling moved the pillow on the couch. No phone. The only things between the seat cushions were a few coins, and under the sofa—dust bunnies. He headed to the steps and heard the shower water running. When Kylee got out, he'd ask her if she'd seen his phone.

Sterling went back to the den. With a sigh, he sat hard and lay back on the couch. The television flickered without sound, but he paid it no mind. Jewel held the full capacity of his focus. With Kylee leaving the next day, he could concentrate on getting Jewel back in his life.

Kylee stayed in the shower so long that Sterling had to call her out. Moments later, she ran back down the steps in lavender polka dot pajamas. The rumble of her feet was thunderous. She plopped beside him. The fresh, clean scent of rose soap clung to her skin.

Kylee laid her head against Sterling's arm. "What time is it, Daddy?"

"Past your bedtime."

"Aw."

The bell rang. Sterling cast a silly inquisitive gaze in Kylee's direction as if she might have known who was there. She sniggered. The sleek silver watch on his arm told him it was close to nine at night. Who could it have been?

The chime permeated the first floor once again.

"Stay right here." Sterling looked at Kylee pointedly. "I'll be right back." Sterling rose as Kylee flicked channels.

Sterling peered through the blinds but couldn't make out the shadow on his porch. He wasn't expecting company. Looking beyond the front yard, he recognized the shape and color of the car that now sat at the curb. His brow knitted.

Hastening to the door, Sterling pulled it open and

stared into Jewel's beautiful face. The face he missed with skin he yearned to touch.

Sterling wanted to ask why she was there but didn't want to sound rude. "Jewel?" Most of all, he didn't want to risk having her turn away.

"Hi." She stepped closer but paused. "Kylee called." She narrowed her eyes inquisitively. "Is everything okay?"

"Yeah…sure." Sterling moved back, gesturing for her to step inside. "Come on in."

Jewel moved like his home was unfamiliar to her. "Is she here?"

"She is." Sterling closed the door. "You said she called you?" Jewel nodded. "Kylee!" Sterling marched toward the den. Jewel followed him.

"Ms. Jewel!" Kylee jumped off the couch and leaped into her arms.

"Hey sweetie!"

"Kylee!" Sterling's voice was firm. Kylee looked down before meeting his chiding gaze. "Ms. Jewel said you called her. Is that true?" At that moment, Sterling noticed his phone on the table in front of the couch. He was certain it wasn't there before.

"Yes, Daddy." Kylee lowered her head.

"Why?" Sterling was clearly puzzled.

"Because you were sad and I missed her, too. I wanted to see her before I left."

Sterling tilted his head and looked at Jewel. With her lips pressed together, she raised both brows.

"I asked if she could please come over as soon as possible."

"Oh honey." Jewel bent forward and squeezed her

cheek. "I thought something was wrong." Jewel explained to Sterling.

Kylee put her head down. Sterling couldn't believe the stunt she pulled but was grateful for it.

"Well she's here now. So say hello and get yourself into bed."

Kylee hugged Jewel's waist. "Thank you for coming. I'm so glad I got to see you before I left." She looked up at Jewel and whispered, "Daddy is glad, too."

"Good night, sweetie." Jewel bent over and hugged Kylee one more time before the happy little girl bounced up the stairs leaving the two behind.

Sterling looked from Kylee's retreating feet to Jewel's stunning face and fought the urge to run the back of his fingers down her cheek. Jewel shifted on her feet and frowned. An awkward air settled between them.

Jewel turned to leave. Sterling reached for her arm. Her body tightened at his touch.

"Don't go." Longing was evident in his voice. Jewel sighed and remained still, but didn't turn to face him. "I've missed you." Sterling hadn't meant to say that aloud. Honesty seeped from him involuntarily. Jewel still hadn't moved. "We need to talk."

Jewel began shaking her head before she spoke. "We shouldn't do this."

"We need to do this." Sterling moved closer, erasing the space between them. Jewel's essence, mixed with her spicy perfume, teased his nostrils. He remembered how much he savored her scent. Instinctively, his eyes closed. He opened them and allowed his gaze to wash over her frame from head to toe. This was his chance—handed to him by his precocious daughter. "I can't sit back and let you walk out of my life. This week without you confirmed for me how much I enjoy being with you. I need to know if you feel the same way."

"Sterling…"

"Answer me, Jewel. Be honest."

Her response was a groan. "Why are you doing this?" she finally asked. "This can't work. Raven…" She huffed. "I heard what she said. She doesn't want me around her daughter. This is why I've always avoided dating men with children. It's not you, Sterling. It's the situation. It can't work."

Sterling remained quiet, waiting for Jewel to finish. "I understand how you feel, but you need to know that Raven doesn't have a problem with you. She was concerned about Kylee. We promised a long time ago to only introduce her to people that we were really serious about and let each other know. I didn't do that. It was my fault. Not yours." Sterling paused to gauge her reaction. He still had her attention. "I knew you needed to come to terms with all of this. When you left I fought with myself all week—contemplating whether or not to let you go. But I don't want to. I have a daughter and an ex-wife. It's not the ideal scenario, but you're the ideal woman for me. This week without you made me realize this even more. I can't just step aside and let you walk away without knowing where I stand. Now I need to know where you stand."

Jewel took a deep breath and took her time releasing it. "I don't know."

"So at least allow us to find out."

Jewel looked to the ceiling and then at Sterling for the first time. He released his hold on her arm. Sterling moved in front of her. He held her chin, closing the space between them. The softness of her lips rekindled his hunger for her. He kissed her again, this time allowing his peck to linger. She remained still, not kissing him back. After another peck, he parted her lips. This time she received him. Sterling wrapped his arms around Jewel, reveling in the feel of her body against his.

Jewel melted inside of his embrace, cupped the side of his face and matched his fervor. They consumed each other—grappling to close the gaps that had widened by their distance in the past week.

Sterling pulled back, looked into her doe eyes and at her kiss-swollen lips. She leaned toward him and initiated the next kiss. Jewel being in his home felt right. His lips belonged on hers.

Sterling planned to kiss away her reservations, love her to contentment and make up for any grief he caused her. With Jewel in his arms, Sterling felt at home in his soul.

Chapter 30

Jewel never thought she'd miss Kylee, but she did. If she felt this way after a few short weeks, Jewel could only imagine how Sterling felt about not having his daughter around. That little girl was wise beyond her years and Jewel was thankful for her wisdom. Because of Kylee, Sterling and Jewel made their way back to each other. Jewel's conversation with Raven at the coffee shop the morning they left for Chicago also helped. Raven had wished them well.

Standing on the balcony, Jewel looked out over the pristine waters of Puerto Rico and let the ocean breeze dance through her hair. This would be the calmest part of her day. She closed her eyes, let her head fall back, and enjoyed the serenity of the moment.

So much had changed in the past few months, most of which Jewel never saw coming. If someone had told her that by the autumn she would have fallen for a man with a child and an ex-wife, she would have laughed in his face. Now she couldn't imagine life without Sterling and Kylee.

Strong arms slid around her waist from behind. She nestled into Sterling's embrace as he pressed his taut chest against her back. The masculine scent of him wafted into her nostrils. Jewel breathed in.

"Beautiful," Sterling said.

"Isn't it?" she agreed.

"I was talking about you."

Jewel shifted in his arms and faced him. "You're not so bad yourself."

Sterling captured her lips. Lately, the simplest touch from him set Jewel's desire in motion. Flinging her arms around him she parted his lips with her tongue and kissed him until both of them were out of breath.

Jewel's phone chirped. Without looking, she knew it was Chloe. After one more peck on Sterling's lips Jewel announced, "We need to go." But Sterling held her tighter.

"What if I don't want to let you go?"

Jewel giggled. "Puerto Rico will have a mad bride on the loose!" She grabbed his hand and led him back into the room.

Together they showered—washing and teasing each other until they could no longer deny their need. Pressing Jewel's back against the shower wall, Sterling lifted her. Instinctively she wrapped her legs around his back and he entered her moist folds. Their bodies collided in a feverish tempo. Jewel moaned. Sterling growled. Her walls clenched around him, cushioning and coaxing a strong climax. Jewel's cries grew louder with each plunge. The edges of her skin tingled. Soon she could no longer stand even his most tender touch. Her release washed over her like floodwaters. The rush of the shower jets muffled her moans. Sterling groaned, thrust and groaned again. His muscles tightened, curling him into her. Grunts rose from his gut with each back-bending compression. At last he pushed as deeply as she would take him and life gushed from him.

For several moments, they held on to each other under the spray of warm water. Their hearts pounded a polyrhythm. Jewel could feel his thumping pulse against her breast. Aftershocks of pure pleasure rumbled through them in spasms. Jewels legs trembled and she licked her lips. She couldn't help it. Sated, she savored the intensity of their connection. It was nothing she'd ever experienced before. Decadent. Powerful. Intense.

Beyond the sound of the shower, Jewel heard her phone faintly in the distance. She looked at Sterling. When their gazes locked they laughed.

"We'd better get out of here," she warned. If they didn't, they would end up starting all over again.

Sterling took her cloth, lathered it up and carefully washed her body. She did the same for him. Minutes later, Jewel rushed from her room with her dress, shoes and accessories in a garment bag.

Serenity was at Chloe's door by the time Jewel reached her sister's room. Jade and their mother were already inside. El steamed Chloe's dress while Jade organized her accessories. Serenity chipped in and helped Jade. Chloe was sitting by the window with the makeup artist wielding a brush over her face. Jewel's jaw dropped when she really looked at Chloe. She'd always though her sister was pretty, but today—her wedding day—she looked stunning. Jewel could only imagine what she'd look like once she was fully dressed.

"Oh my goodness. Chloe. You look so beautiful!" Jewel covered her mouth. Tears stung her eyes.

"Don't make me cry, Jewel." Chloe batted her eyes, waving her hands like a fan to keep them dry.

"I'm sorry. I can't help it." Tears rolled down Jewel's face. She swiped them. "My big sister is getting married!"

"I know," Jade squealed.

Always collected, El simply smiled while her girls engaged in a mini scream fest.

"Okay. Don't mess up your mascara, lady." Jewel handed Chloe a tissue. The makeup artist skillfully worked around her.

The next moments were a flurry of adjusting under-garments, pulling dresses over their heads and seeking out single shoes. When El and the girls were all ready, they helped Chloe into her dress—a strapless number that hugged her curves in front and billowed past her ankles in the back. Her perfect bun was topped with a ring of white flowers. Serenity, El, Jade and Jewel stepped back and admired Chloe when she was done.

"Simply beautiful."

"Stunning."

"Gorgeous."

Each had a word for her, but El was quiet. Jewel looked over and her mother's lip trembled. El clasped her hands together, shook her head and allowed tears to roll down her face.

"Ma!" Chloe pouted.

El shrugged. "My baby is getting married," she said, abolishing every dry eye in the room.

There was a knock at the door and the girls got themselves together.

"Who is it?" Jade opened the door before anyone could answer.

Chloe's bridal attendant, assigned by their wedding

coordinator, led them down to where Chloe would emerge to cross the sand and meet her awaiting husband-to-be.

The hotel grounds were as stunning as the bride, with large, lush tropical greenery expertly placed throughout the space. Jewel looked to the other side of the infinity pool and spotted the men waiting under a lovely arch in the sand.

The attendant nodded and music floated into the atmosphere. Donovan stood next to his brother, Dayton, and Chris was next to him. The men took their places under the arch to get ready for the ceremony. Chloe was led to Bobby Dale who took her arm in his. Together they walked across the pearly white sand, closer to the water. Chloe seemed to glide. Donovan appeared to be in awe of the sight of his bride.

Jade and Jewel walked in first, clearing the path for Chloe. Unable to see far beyond her tears, Jewel smiled at her presumed family members as she passed them. When she and Jade took their positions under the arch, the music stopped. Their cousin Kendal, a well-known pop singer, stood and positioned herself near the front. Serenity picked up her violin and stood beside her. Together, they serenaded Chloe and Bobby Dale down the aisle. Kendal's popular love song accompanied by the delightful melody floating from Serenity's violin added to the beauty of the setting.

Donovan, looking more handsome than Jewel ever remembered, stepped up to receive his fiancée from Bobby Dale's embrace. They seemed to stare beyond each other's eyes and into their souls. The fullness of their admiration oozed into the atmosphere, mesmerizing the guests. Jewel couldn't help but smile. She knew what it was like to look someone in the eyes and nearly drown in your love for them.

Wait! Had she just said love? Jewel looked out over the small gathering of family and friends and spotted Sterling. His gaze was already locked on her. Sterling winked and that sexy side-cocked smile of his made her warm on the inside as if he'd physically touched her.

So that's what it was. She loved him. It was love that made her want to share every idea and accomplishment with him. It was love that gave her the courage to meet the other love of his life—Kylee. It was love that caused her body to tingle from a simple touch. It was love that was starved and craved Sterling's rich voice, scent and affection when they were apart. And it was love that just wouldn't allow her to walk away when she thought what they had wouldn't work because of his past.

It was also love that led her back to him that night when Kylee called. The realization hit her like a falling wall of bricks. Jewel could pinpoint when it happened, but she knew for sure that she loved Sterling and hoped he felt the same. Jewel's concentration faded in and out while Chloe and Donovan exchanged the vows they wrote. Applause exploded when Donovan kissed the bride and the Rivers were announced to the guests for the first time.

Jewel was happy for them, but this notion of love took her focus. Was it really love? she wondered. It must be.

The wedding party was being whisked away to take pictures with the newlyweds against breathtaking backdrops. Jewel smiled, but her mind was on Sterling. Her discovery made her long to be near him. She had to find a way to gauge how he felt about her. Of course he had strong feelings, too. Jewel didn't doubt that. His actions were clear, but did he love her?

Jewel concentrated hard on being in the moment for Chloe's sake. She'd get to Sterling soon enough. Those notions of love could be from being caught up in the wedding festivities.

When the pictures were done, they joined the rest of their family and friends in the banquet hall for the reception. Jewel, Dayton, Jade, Chris and finally Chloe and Donovan were announced as they entered the room. Immediately after, Kendal took to the microphone once again and sang as Donovan and Chloe shared their first dance. Mr. and Mrs. Rivers along with El and Bobby Dale joined them. Other couples were also invited to the floor.

"Can I have this dance?" Sterling whispered in Jewel's ear from behind.

Goose bumps lined her arms at the sound of his voice and the heat of his breath on her. The way her body responded to him tickled her.

"I'd love to dance with you."

Sterling eased one arm around her waist and held her hand with the other as they swayed to the music.

"I didn't think it was possible for you to look more beautiful."

"Who me?" Jewel gave a coy shrug.

"Ha! Yes, you. That sense of humor." Sterling laughed. "What about it?"

"It's one of the many things I love about you."

Jewel missed a step. "You love that about me?" She willed her heart to stop trying to thump out of her chest.

"Yes. I do."

"Do you mind sharing some of the other things you say you love about me?"

"Your ambition, your determination, your wittiness,

the fact that you know how to have fun, the cute little way you bite your bottom lip when we make love."

Jewel gasped and then looked around making sure no one was close enough to hear his last comment before snickering.

"There's a lot. I just love you!"

Jewel stopped moving altogether. "What did you just say?"

"I. Love. You."

Jewel thought she would explode into millions of tiny, happy little pieces. "Oh my goodness, Sterling! I love you, too!"

His smile was easy, confident, as if he'd been waiting for Jewel to come around. Now he stopped moving and studied her. Their eyes locked in an adoring gaze. She felt it on the inside. Sterling's stare intensified.

"Jewel," Sterling's smile vanished. His expression became serious. "I've loved you for a while now. I was just waiting for you to catch up."

"I'm here now."

Sterling took her face in his hands and kissed her so passionately Jewel felt as if she'd been lifted from the ground.

Standards. Jewel thought about her list and how dating Sterling had broken all of her rules. Both he and Kylee had completely seized her heart. With his lips against hers she couldn't imagine being anywhere else but in his arms...forever.

* * * * *

KIMANI™
ROMANCE

COMING NEXT MONTH
Available May 22, 2018

#573 WHEN I'M WITH YOU
The Lawsons of Louisiana • by Donna Hill

Longtime New Orleans bachelor Rafe Lawson is ready to tie the knot.
His heart has been captured by the gorgeous Avery Richards. Then the media
descends, jeopardizing her Secret Service career—and their imminent wedding.
But it's the unexpected return of Rafe's first love that could cost the tycoon
everything.

#574 PLEASURE IN HIS KISS
Love in the Hamptons • by Pamela Yaye

Beauty blogger and owner of the Hamptons's hottest salon Karma Sullivan
has been swept off her feet by judge Morrison Drake. But she knows their
passion-filled nights must end. She can't let her family secret derail Morrison's
ambitious career plan. Even if it means giving up the man she loves…

#575 TEMPTING THE BEAUTY QUEEN
Once Upon a Tiara • by Carolyn Hector

If Kenzie Swayne didn't require a date for a string
of upcoming weddings, she'd turn Ramon Torres's
offer down flat. The gorgeous entrepreneur stood
her up once already. Now Ramon needs Kenzie's
expertise for a new business venture. But when
past secrets are revealed, can Ramon make Kenzie
his—forever?

#576 WHEREVER YOU ARE
The Jacksons of Ann Arbor • by Elle Wright

Avery Montgomery created a hit show about her
old neighborhood, but she can't reveal the real
reason she left town. Dr. Elwood Jackson has never
forgiven Avery for leaving. But when a crisis lands
her in El's emergency room, passion sparks hotter
than before. Will this be their second chance?

Get 2 Free Books,
Plus 2 Free Gifts—
just for trying the
Reader Service!

YES! Please send me 2 FREE Harlequin® Kimani™ Romance novels and my 2 FREE gifts (gifts are worth about $10 retail). After receiving them, if I don't wish to receive any more books, I can return the shipping statement marked "cancel." If I don't cancel, I will receive 4 brand-new novels every month and be billed just $5.69 per book in the U.S. or $6.24 per book in Canada. That's a savings of at least 12% off the cover price. It's quite a bargain! Shipping and handling is just 50¢ per book in the U.S. and 75¢ per book in Canada*. I understand that accepting the 2 free books and gifts places me under no obligation to buy anything. I can always return a shipment and cancel at any time. The free books and gifts are mine to keep no matter what I decide.

168/368 XDN GMWW

Name	(PLEASE PRINT)	
Address		Apt. #
City	State/Prov.	Zip/Postal Code

Signature (if under 18, a parent or guardian must sign)

Mail to the **Reader Service:**
IN U.S.A.: P.O. Box 1341, Buffalo, NY 14240-8531
IN CANADA: P.O. Box 603, Fort Erie, Ontario L2A 5X3

Want to try two free books from another line?
Call 1-800-873-8635 or visit www.ReaderService.com.

*Terms and prices subject to change without notice. Prices do not include applicable taxes. Sales tax applicable in NY. Canadian residents will be charged applicable taxes. Offer not valid in Quebec. This offer is limited to one order per household. Books received may not be as shown. Not valid for current subscribers to Harlequin® Kimani™ Romance books. All orders subject to approval. Credit or debit balances in a customer's account(s) may be offset by any other outstanding balance owed by or to the customer. Please allow 4 to 6 weeks for delivery. Offer available while quantities last.

Your Privacy—The Reader Service is committed to protecting your privacy. Our Privacy Policy is available online at www.ReaderService.com or upon request from the Reader Service.

We make a portion of our mailing list available to reputable third parties that offer products we believe may interest you. If you prefer that we not exchange your name with third parties, or if you wish to clarify or modify your communication preferences, please visit us at www.ReaderService.com/consumerschoice or write to us at Reader Service Preference Service, P.O. Box 9062, Buffalo, NY 14240-9062. Include your complete name and address.

KROM17R3

They were a natural fit with each other, as if living under
the same roof was something they'd always done. Rafe
was attentive, but gave her space. He possessed chef-like
skills in the kitchen, a penchant for neatness—she never
had to step over discarded clothing or clean up after a
meal—and above all he was a master in the bedroom and
made her see heaven on a regular basis. This man was
going to be her husband. Sometimes, when she looked
at him or held him tight between her thighs, she couldn't
believe that Rafe Lawson was hers. What she wanted was
just the two of them, but marrying Rafe was marrying
his large, controlling family.

"You sure you'll be okay until I get back from N'awlins?" He wiped off the countertop with a damp cloth.

She shimmied onto the bar stool at the island counter and extended her hands to Rafe. He took two long steps and was in front of her. He raised her hands to his lips and kissed the insides of her palms.

"I'll be fine, and right here when you get back." She leaned in to kiss him.

"Hmm, I can change my plans," he said against her lips, "and stay here, which is what I'd rather do." He caressed her hips.

Avery giggled. "Me, too, but you've been gone long enough. Take care of your business."

He stepped deep between her legs. "Business can wait." He threaded his fingers through the hair at the nape of her neck, dipped his head and kissed her collarbone.

Avery sucked in a breath of desire and instinctively tightened her legs around him. "You're going to be late," she whispered.

He brushed his lips along her neck, nibbled the lobe of her ear. "Privilege is the perk of owning your own plane. Can't leave without me."

Don't miss WHEN I'M WITH YOU
by Donna Hill, available June 2018
wherever Harlequin® Kimani Romance™ books
and ebooks are sold.

"Why did you leave your service revolver on my bathroom
counter?" Armstrong asked as they stood at the bus stop, waiting
for her return ride.

"I can't risk keeping it strapped on me and I was afraid one of
the girls might go through my bag and find it. I knew it was safe
with you."

"I don't like you not having your gun."

"I'll be fine. I have a black belt in karate and jujitsu. I know how
to take care of myself!"

Armstrong nodded. "So you keep telling me. It doesn't mean
I'm not going to worry about you, though."

Danni rocked back and forth on her heels. Deep down she was
grateful that a man did care. For longer than she wanted to admit,
there hadn't been a man who did.

Armstrong interrupted her thoughts. "There's a protective detail
already in front of the coffee shop and another that will follow you
and your bus. There will be someone on you at all times. If you get
into any trouble, you know what to do."

Danni nodded. "I'll contact you as soon as it's feasible. And
please, if there is any change in Alissa's condition, find a way to

let me know."

"I will. I promise."

Danni's attention shifted to the bus that had turned the corner and was making its way toward them. A wave of sadness suddenly rippled through her stomach.

"You good?" Armstrong asked, sensing the change in her mood.

She nodded, biting back the rise of emotion. "I'll be fine," she answered.

As the bus pulled up to the stop, he drew her hand into his and pulled it to his mouth, kissing the backs of her fingers.

Danni gave him one last smile as she fell into line with the others boarding the bus. She tossed a look over her shoulder as he stood staring after her. The woman in front of her was pushing an infant in a stroller. A boy about eight years old and a little girl about five clung to each side of the carriage. The little girl looked back at Danni and smiled before hiding her face in her mother's skirt. The line stopped, an elderly woman closer to the front struggling with a multitude of bags to get inside.

She suddenly spun around, the man behind her eyeing her warily. "Excuse me," she said as she pushed past him and stepped aside. She called after Armstrong as she hurried back to where he stood.

"What's wrong?" he said as she came to a stop in front of him

"Nothing," Danni said as she pressed both palms against his broad chest. "Nothing at all." She lifted herself up on her toes as her gaze locked with his. Her hands slid up his chest to the sides of his face. She gently cupped her palms against his cheeks and then she pressed her lips to his.

Don't miss
SEDUCED BY THE BADGE by Deborah Fletcher Mello,
available June 2018 wherever
Harlequin® Romantic Suspense books and ebooks are sold.

www.Harlequin.com

Need an adrenaline rush from nail-biting tales
(and irresistible males)?

Check out **Harlequin® Intrigue®**
and **Harlequin® Romantic Suspense** books!

New books available every month!

CONNECT WITH US AT:

Harlequin.com/Community

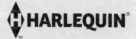

Facebook.com/HarlequinBooks

Twitter.com/HarlequinBooks

Instagram.com/HarlequinBooks

Pinterest.com/HarlequinBooks

ReaderService.com

 HARLEQUIN®

**ROMANCE WHEN
YOU NEED IT**

SGENRE2017